In Pawnee, the Law Stands Alone!

He came even with the first corner of the place, where the shadow lay black and heavy. And it was from this darkened angle that the flame of a gun and the hard, heavy note of it lashed out at him, while the shock of the bullet sent him staggering.

He was spinning, clawing for his own weapon, when still another voice—this time a human one—struck out also, cold and toneless. The voice of Harry Shelline, tinhorn gambler and killer.

"Takes more than words, Allard, to run me out of town—and make it stick."

Then the gun flamed again....

PAYOFF AT PAWNEE

L. P. Holmes

WARNER BOOKS

A Warner Communications Company

WARNER BOOKS EDITION

Copyright ©1981 by L. P. Holmes
All rights reserved.

Warner Books, Inc.
75 Rockefeller Plaza
New York, N.Y. 10019

W A Warner Communications Company

Printed in the United States of America

First Warner Books Printing: August, 1985

10 9 8 7 6 5 4 3 2 1

PAYOFF
AT PAWNEE

CHAPTER ONE

FRANK ALLARD had his first look at this town of Pawnee through the cold discomfort of the late spring rain which slanted down out of the cloud-shrouded, high country to the north. In what had passed for sleep, he had spent last night slumped in a round-backed chair in the dingy barroom of the old stage station at Lompoc, some thirty miles to the south. The half-dollar he had spent this morning for a greasy breakfast, served by a sullen half-breed with a knife-scarred face, was the last cent he had in his jeans. That had been many hours ago. Now he knew hunger again, and the chilled stiffness which came from riding weary miles into the teeth of this wind-driven, relentless downpour.

His slicker was old, the life long since gone out of it. And though it was buttoned to his chin, the rain's searching wetness had worked through in many places and laid a clammy, dismal touch across both his shoulders and chest and down the shrinking, knotted muscles in the hollow of his lean belly. Water in a steady cascade drained from the sloppy sodden brim of his hat. Twice in the past hour he had tried to achieve the frugal comfort of a cigarette, but between the rain and the nagging wind and the fumbling of his cold-stiffened fingers, flimsy papers had torn and tobacco had sifted away. So he cursed in weary disgust and let it go at that.

The storm's murk was hastening day's end and lights were already beginning to show in Pawnee, their glow thin and yellow and almost furtive in the gloom. A locomotive whistle bayed in loneliness and a five-car freight went rumbling and clanking into the east. The smell of coal smoke and oily steam rode on the wind. Heavy also was another odor, the stench of wet cattle pens and loading yards.

Allard put his gaunt and weary roan across the tracks and reined into the end of a street that stretched raggedly westward. He rode along this at a slow, slogging walk, the pace of a horse and a man both thoroughly trail-worn. There were few active signs of life about—just a rig or two and a thin scattering of cow ponies here and there along the hitch rails, humped and patient, rumps turned to the wind's wet and nagging pressure. Down the street a couple of human figures showed momentarily, moving from one doorway to duck into another, and the echo of a man's fretful, cursing complaint drifted back.

On the south side of the street a two-story building lifted gaunt, square shoulders. A porch ran the full length of this, its roof a balcony for the second story. An out-jutting joist carried a swinging sign, which creaked thinly as the wind jostled it. Allard reined up under the sign, squinting against the drive of the rain as he spelled out the words in the uncertain, fading light.

GIL PAXTON, GEN'L MDSE.

Allard nodded to himself, put the roan in to the hitch rail, and swung stiffly from his saddle. He stood for a moment with a hand against the roan's wet shoulder, steadying himself until his numbed feet got full feel of the sodden earth. Just beyond the roan was a spring wagon and team, the bed of the wagon covered with a tied-down tarp. One corner of this had worked loose and was flapping in the wind.

Allard's glance touched the wagon, moved on, then came swiftly back. The tarp, wet from the storm, had sagged down, vaguely outlining something that lay beneath it. There was a grisly suggestion in that outline. Allard moved a little closer for a better look. A gust of wind seized the loose corner of the tarp, twisted it, and flung it back. A booted foot was disclosed, the toe pointing upward and out in a way grimly significant.

It was a jolting discovery and a bleak introduction to this town of Pawnee. Allard moved back a stride and his head lifted, his glance again probing the long reach of the darkening street. Somberness burned in his deep-set eyes and his lips thinned with sudden pressure. He turned and climbed the low steps of the porch and for the first time in the long, dreary run of the day, found shelter from the rain's persistence.

The door of the store opened and three people came out. Two were men, one a bulky figure in a hip length canvas coat, the other short, on the stout side, bareheaded and in vest and shirt-sleeves. The third of the group was a young woman, her erectness swathed from chin to ankles in a yellow slicker. She was settling a flat-crowned Stetson firmly on her head and pulling the throat thong snug against the whip of the wind. The stout man in vest and shirt-sleeves was arguing earnestly.

"Wish you'd change your mind, Barbara. It'd be a longdrive out to the ranch alone on a night like this one shaping up, even if the wagon was empty."

The girl did not answer, moving out to the edge of the porch. The bulky man in the canvas coat now added his bit.

"Just say the word, Miss Chancellor, and I'll have Con Waters drive you home."

The girl turned then, and the thin, yellow glow of the store lights struck through the open door. Frank Allard, standing quietly there to one side, saw that strain and pallor lay in this girl's cheeks, and when she spoke he heard a voice that was low and freighted with a tautness that told of emotions under tight rein.

"Flick Lester and I rode to town together. We will ride home together. And if there was another point of supply within a hundred miles, neither I nor any of my riders would ever show in this miserable town again. You've been promising us a better town, but it hasn't changed a bit. It is still the same murderous hole, and Pinto Jardene still owns it. Owns the town, its thugs, and what passes as law!"

Both men shifted restlessly under the bitter lash of her words. The one in the canvas coat gave a rather blustering answer. "Now that's hardly fair, Miss Chancellor. Gil Paxton here, and me—we're both mighty sorry about Flick Lester. But truth is, he forced the trouble and the gunplay. On the spot witnesses swear that Harry Shelline shot in self-defense. And I can't hold a man for that."

"Harry Shelline!" There was a rising note of ragged and loosening emotion in the girl's voice. "A cheap, crooked gambler! It's the same old story, the same shameless excuse. You'd have me believe that all of Pawnee is sorry, wouldn't you! What good does that do when a man is shot down just because he wouldn't stand for being robbed by a filthy gambler? But Pinto Jardene and the men he owns are never at fault, are they? Oh no, of course not! So they go on cheating and killing and getting away with it...!"

She seemed to choke up, for she pressed a slim hand to her throat. Abruptly she whirled, went down the steps in a quick rush, ducked under the hitch rail, and tugged at the halter ropes of the spring wagon team. A moment later she was up on the seat of the rig, a brake rod clanked and squealed, and then the wagon swung out and rolled down the street, turning abruptly to the left and disappearing into a crossway.

The rain beat down, the store sign swung in the wind and creaked its dismal complaint. The stout man in shirt-sleeves cleared his throat harshly.

"Twelve miles in weather like this—and a dead man riding the bed of the wagon. Mosby, that girl's got more courage than a lot of men. And she's right about this town. This goddamned town! Some of the people in it are getting harder to swallow every day. I suggest you have a damned straight talk with Pinto Jardene about his pet house man, Mister Harry Shelline."

Lee Mosby shrugged his canvas-clad shoulders and spat out into the rain. "I'm running this town the way most people want it run, you included, Gil. It's a matter of business with all you fellows. You like the sight and feel of the money that comes in with these trail crews. And you either give those men the kind of town they like to spend their money in, or they don't spend it here. Simple as that!"

The storekeeper folded his arms, hugging himself against the dank chill while he stared along the deepening gloom of the street. He spoke with a slow soberness that had troubled thoughts behind it.

"All of which has nothing to do with Harry Shelline gunning Flick Lester, a rider from one of the biggest of the Bench outfits. You know, Mosby, before the trail

11

herds ever began driving here to ship, this town of Pawnee had to live off the trade that came down from the Bench. And when the trail herds from the south quit coming here—as they will one of these days—then Pawnee will be right back depending on Bench trade. The folks from up there are our past and our future. The trail outfits are only the present."

"That may be," agreed Mosby. "But the present is now and where I live. Also, Gil, you want to remember that some of the Bench riders are hardly gentle angels. And I tell you, Flick Lester forced that gunplay. He lost a few dollars at Shelline's table, got soreheaded, and charged Shelline with crooked dealing. Then he went for his gun and just wasn't fast enough. Hell, man! Would you expect Shelline to just sit there like a dumb fool and let Lester put lead into him?"

"It would have been small loss if Lester had got there first," Paxton said dryly. "I don't doubt a bit that Shelline was dealing a crooked game. He's a professional gambler and, in spite of what some misguided people might think, there's no such thing as a square professional gambler. I've seen a lot of such in my time and never ran across one yet who wouldn't go to the bottom of the deck any time he thought he could get away with it. They're strictly in the business to win, and Shelline is no exception."

Mosby shrugged again. "I don't know anything about that. But I do know that this latest ruckus is no fault of mine. For I can't be on duty night and day and everywhere at once. Oh, had I happened to be in the Palace at the time, I might have headed things off. But I was at the office, trying to catch up on a little sleep against another stretch of night duty. After all a man's got the right to some sleep once in awhile. So if you fellows want the town run tighter than it is now, then get together and round me up a good night man, like you've been promising me for so long."

"When the right man comes along, Lee—you'll have

him," Paxton said. "But it's not easy finding a man who takes to that sort of work and is capable of handling it right."

"I savvy that," Mosby agreed. "But as things stand now I'm doing my best. And I just can't get around to wet-nursing every stray puncher who sits into a game and then goes shooting crazy just because he's dropped a few dollars. I got too many other troubles."

From the far eastern end of the street where the bulk of the town's lights shone like yellow surface gleams in the eyes of a surly animal, lights advertising dives and deadfalls, there lifted a high, wild, drunken yell, followed by the dull, heavy thud of a gun shot. Mosby jerked around, listened a moment, then dropped quickly down the store steps and set off at a plunging, forward-leaning walk that was almost a run, tossing blunt, sarcastic words over his shoulder.

"See what I mean, Gil?"

The storekeeper stared after Mosby, then said again, "This goddamned town—!" He turned and stamped into the store.

Frank Allard followed him in, stopping just inside the door. Water dribbled down his slicker and shone wetly in the light of the store's three hanging lamps. Allard took off his hat, whipped it back and forth, scattering moisture. Gil Paxton turned with a professionally impersonal glance.

"Something I can do for you?"

Allard unbuttoned his slicker, shrugged out of it, dropped it to the floor. He thrust his hands under his armpits, scrubbed them up and down to dry them. Then, from an inner pocket, he brought out a crumpled envelope and offered it to Paxton, who glanced at it, took out the enclosure and skimmed through it with just a fleeting look. Then his eyes came back to this rangy, storm-whipped man with a quickening interest.

"You're Frank Allard?"

"That's right." Allard moved over to the pleasantly

13

muttering stove which stood in the center of the big room. He spread his hands to the welcome heat. Gil Paxton, still studying him, spoke slowly.

"Under the circumstances, I've got to make sure. No offense intended, you understand. But when you set out to fulfill the trust of a dead man, you owe it to him to be careful."

"Of course." Allard tipped his head slightly.

"What sort of man was Jim Creightly?" asked Paxton. "For instance, what did he look like? What were his mannerisms?"

"He stood about as tall as you," Allard said. "But he was lean and wiry, cat light on his feet. He had black hair and eyes, and when he left the Lodgepole River country he was wearing a small mustache and imperial, which made him look older than he was. He was twenty-nine. He had the knack of making friends because he laughed easy and got a lot of fun out of life. He never hunted trouble, but he could handle his share of it if it showed. His gun was horn-gripped and he carried it hip high on the left side. He could handle that, too, with a cross body draw that was poison fast, so whoever it was that shot him, must have got him in the back, or at a time when he had no idea of the other fellow's intentions."

"Let's see your left hand," said Paxton. "The back of it."

Allard held it out. It was a solid, strong hand with a small lump on the back of it where the metacarpal bone below the second finger had been broken at some time past. Gil Paxton had his look, then nodded, satisfied.

"You pass, Allard. The money is yours. I have it in my safe, yonder. This letter—I wrote it and you produced it, which perhaps was proof enough in itself. But there was always the chance."

"Of course," Allard said again. "I understand. You had every right to make sure of me."

Paxton went over to his safe, opened it, and brought out a compact canvas sack which bulged and clinked heavily as he dropped it on the store counter.

"There it is, all thirty-four hundred dollars of it, just as Jim Creightly gave it to me to hold for him. It was only a few days later that he was shot. I was lucky enough to have a moment or two with him before he died. He told me about you being his partner and where a letter would reach you. He asked me to hold the money for you, and I promised that I would. When I asked him for some sure way I could identify you, all he could manage to tell me about was that knot on the back of your left hand. He was sinking fast at the time so I couldn't press him for any more details." Paxton was untying the mouth of the sack while he spoke. "You can count it."

"No need of that," said Allard in his terse, quiet way. "I'll take a couple of hundred now because I'm flat broke. The rest, you put back in your safe. You held it for Jim Creightly, you can hold it for me. And if it should happen that I'm not able to come in here and claim it at some future time, then it's all yours for your trouble. For there is nobody else. Jim and I ran things just between the two of us."

Paxton watched Allard count out ten double eagles from the sack, the gold coins shining in the lamplight. He was watching a rangy, big-shouldered man who had that certain ruggedness that solid, heavy bones supplied. This same ruggedness marked a face that was broad across the cheekbones and strong of jaw. The nose was high-bridged, a little hawkish, and under this the mouth was wide, with a certain faint pull of harshness at the corners. Cold blue eyes were deep set and so unwaveringly steady, they seemed to carry an actual impact.

Allard spoke again, abruptly. "I'll go further. Name me the man who shot Jim Creightly and all this money is yours, right now!"

15

Paxton's reply held a thread of curtness. "If I knew, you wouldn't have to buy the information from me. Creightly had no idea about that, either. It was the first thing I asked him. And he didn't know."

Allard considered this for one long moment, his deep eyes coldly brooding. "Got time to tell me what you know about the shooting?"

Paxton hoisted himself to the counter, sat there for some little time in reflection.

"It was at night," he said presently. "Around eight o'clock as I recall. The herd Creightly brought in had been shipped some four days previous, and the buyer, Pollack, had paid off in gold. Creightly settled up with the saddle hands who'd helped him work the drive, then brought the rest of the money to me to hold for him until he was ready to leave town."

"What happened to the riders who had come in with Jim?" Allard asked.

Paxton showed a small shrug. "After the shooting I tried to locate some of them, but they had all scattered. You know how most of these trail hands are. They get paid off at the end of a drive, have their fling in the dives, then drift. You'd know more about them than I would, having seen them pull out with Creightly at the start of the drive."

Allard nodded. "They were just pickup hands. Jim and I weren't big enough to afford a steady crew. Our outfit was strictly a two-man deal. Now about that shooting—?"

"As I say," went on Paxton, "it was night, early. I was thinking about closing up when I heard this lone shot out in the street. I went out on the porch and heard somebody running upstreet, that would be west, as I call it. It was one of those black dark nights, and I wasn't able to see a damn thing. But for some reason I had a queer feeling about the affair, so I went out and prowled the street a bit. I practically stumbled over Jim Creightly, lying there. Con Waters had heard the shot, too, and he came out of his livery barn to investigate. The two of us carried Creightly into this store and while I did what I could for him, Con Waters went after Doctor Sanchez."

Paxton stared at the floor, brooding over the memory. Presently he went on. "Doctor Sanchez needed only a glance to see that Jim Creightly didn't have a chance. He gave him a stimulant of some sort that held him together long enough to answer a few questions, like who had shot him and what to do about the money. I've told you what he could and did answer to these. A little later he died. That's the all of it."

"You say you heard somebody running away from the shooting, but you couldn't make out who it was?" probed Allard.

"That's right. It was a thick night, just too damn dark."

"This cattle buyer, Pollock you named him—what sort was he?"

Paxton pulled at pursed lips with thumb and forefinger. "I'd call him a reliable man. He made a clean deal with Creightly and paid off promptly with gold."

"Has he been here in Pawnee since Jim was killed?"

"Some. He buys for Lord & McKeever and is a pretty busy man, in and out of town a great deal. You'll probably see him around."

Allard went silent, his face bleakly taciturn. "Pretty much a blind trail, looks like," he said presently. "Damned little to go on."

"Then you intend trying to do something about it?"

Allard's head came up and his voice ran harsh. "It wasn't just the money that brought me here to Pawnee. Jim Creightly was my best friend and my partner. So maybe if I stick around and look long and hard enough, I may pick up the trail."

"Understand exactly how you feel," agreed Paxton. "But I wouldn't know where or how to tell you to start."

Eyes pinched with thought, Allard mused on this.

"Somebody who knew Jim had been paid off for a herd could have figured to grab the money, so they shot him in the back while making a try for it."

"I rummaged around with that thought myself," said Paxton. "But somehow it just didn't add up. Because thirty-four hundred dollars in gold would be quite a load for any man to carry around casually. And Creightly wasn't carrying it."

"You got any other ideas you'd care to offer? I'd be obliged."

Paxton slid down off the counter. "I've played with a dozen of them, and none of them added up to much hard sense. So anything I'd have to offer would be just a guess of the emptiest kind. For that matter, Creightly could have been killed by mistake, mistaken for somebody else mixed up in some kind of undercurrent feud coming out of one of the dives. Such things have happened before. This town—this damned town! Once it was a good town, but no longer. Now anything can happen in it."

Allard stared into his frustrated thoughts for a time, then ran his glance along the store shelves. "I'll be around for a time and I need some new clothes. And what would you recommend in the way of a room?"

"Ben Ripon's Trail View Hotel is as good as any." Paxton returned the sack of money to the safe, then looked Allard up and down with an expertly measuring eye and began laying out the required clothes from well-stocked shelves.

Now that his hands were dry and warm again, Allard twisted up his long-denied cigarette. Through a mouthful of smoke he spoke slowly.

"Listened in on what you and that fellow Mosby had to say outside. I take it he's the town marshal. He was asking for a night man to help him with his job, and you admitted he could use one. Still feel that way about it?"

This brought Paxton up, straight and startled. "You mean you might be interested?"

"Offer me the job, and see."

Again Gil Paxton measured this rangy, cold-jawed rider with the deep, almost harshly intent eyes. "You've the look of being able to take care of yourself," he admitted. "But I warn you, it's a thankless prospect. For no matter which way you move you'll be wrong in the eyes of some. There are politics in this town, and at times they can be pretty damned low politics. Then again there's always the chance that some crazy gun-hand might—"

"I know," cut in Allard. "But I still want the job if I can get it."

"You're asking for a job you don't need. From what you've said, your big interest is running down the trail of the man who shot Jim Creightly. You figure that being night marshal might help you there?"

"That's right. I'd have legitimate entry into every dive and deadfall in town without arousing suspicion, as I might if I was just another drifter hanging around town and asking questions. I could look and listen and form my judgment of men. And somewhere, maybe a chance word or unguarded remark I'd pick up ...well..." Allard finished with a shrug.

The storekeeper nodded soberly. "That is so. Well, I'll see what I can do. I haven't the full say-so, you understand. I do have some say in the running of the town's affairs, but there are others who will have to pass on the deal. I'll sound them out and let you know."

Allard gathered up his purchases and wrapped a new slicker around them. "Might be smart not to mention my connection with Jim Creightly. At least not until I get my roots set. After that," and harshness roughened his tone again, "it won't matter much. It might even start somebody sweating."

"That would be wise," conceded Paxton. "In this town it is wise to be silent about many things. And for that reason it wouldn't be smart for Con Waters and me to seek you out at the hotel. You'll be putting your horse up at Con's livery barn, I imagine? Well, after you've had your supper I suggest you drift down to Con's layout as though checking up on how your horse is being taken care of. Then we'll see."

There was a stairway at one end of the store, leading up to the second story. Now, as Frank Allard turned to leave, steps sounded and a feminine figure moved off the stairs and out where the store lights could touch her.

"Supper's ready," she called.

Allard flashed a quick glance at her and saw a sturdy, deep-bosomed girl in a kitchen apron. She had dark hair and eyes and an oval, pretty face. But about her full red lips there were the pouting lines of a rebellious, almost sullen discontent.

As Allard moved on, he heard Paxton answer, "I'll be right along, Nell!"

Outside the wind was still pushing a burly way around, but the rain had slackened to a misty drizzle. Allard led his drenched and weary roan over to the livery barn, arranged for the care of the animal, then plodded up the soggy street to the Trail View Hotel.

Ben Ripon, who ran the place, was a leathery little man with bright, quick eyes, big ears, and a tuft of grizzled hair which stood up on his head like a scalp lock. He watched Frank Allard sign the register, then indicated a room.

"I could stand a hot bath," Allard told him. "And after that, some grub."

Ben Ripon ducked his head. "Bathroom at the end of the hall. I'll have Chigger bring you some hot water. Supper in half an hour. Going to be with us long?"

Allard seemed to consider this possibility with speculative thought. After which he shrugged laconically. "Depends."

Chigger was a squat and silent half-breed and reasonably generous with the hot water. Allard had brought a meager warbag up to the hotel with him and from this he dug out razor and soap. He shaved, then soaked and scrubbed and steamed in deep comfort, and grew thoroughly warm again all through. He bundled his old clothes and told Chiggar to throw them away. He dressed and went down to the hotel dining room, ate to repletion, bought a couple of cigars at the hotel bar, then returned to his room.

From his warbag he brought forth a heavy Colt gun that had been wrapped in an oily cloth. He inspected the weapon, spun the cylinder a couple of times, and then from a partly emptied box of cartridges, filled five chambers of the cylinder with fat, yellow loads, lowered the hammer on the empty sixth chamber, and tucked the weapon inside the waistband of his jeans, a little around to the left side. He donned a new, fleece-lined canvas coat, buttoned it, turned the collar up, then went quietly out into the street, a taciturn man with the glint of cold purpose in his eyes.

CHAPTER TWO

CON WATERS, who owned and ran the livery barn and corrals, was a thin, wiry Irishman with rusty hair and shrewd, level eyes. He and Gil Paxton were huddled over a small, cast-iron stove in a corner room of the stable. There was a bunk, a table, and a couple of chairs. A low-turned lamp on the table fought the gloom back with fair success. On the stove a battered tea kettle hissed and whispered.

There was a hint of reservation in Con Waters' handshake at Gil Paxton's introduction, and in the shadowed light Frank Allard could feel the Irishman's glance measuring him carefully.

"Now then," said Waters, "Gil here tells me you're willing to take on with us as night marshal, Mister Allard. For reasons of your own, of course?"

Allard tipped his head. "That's right."

Waters backed up to the stove again, put his hands behind him. "That's all right, too," he observed. "What any man does is generally for reasons of his own. But before I put my full approval on this matter I'll have to know that you're willing to go a little further than that."

Allard's eyes pinched down a trifle. "Meaning—what?"

Con Waters seemed to settle himself more firmly on his spread feet. "It's this way, Mister Allard. Men like Gil Paxton and myself have seen this town of Pawnee grow since it was nothing more than half a dozen sod shanties. We like to feel that we helped build it, and that we built it on the principle of fair trading and a square deal, so that it might win the friendship and confidence of decent folk, like most of the ranchers from the Bench range. In time the railroad came and after that the trail herds. And that would still have been all right."

The stable owner freshened his pipe with a match before going on.

"Now I think I can claim to being a practical man and no shouting reformist or hypocrite. The land hereabouts is a lusty one and the men who live in it are lusty men who like their pleasures so. And I've still no quarrel with such conditions providing they are honest. But there are those who have come into our town who offer it neither honesty nor decency. Men like Pinto Jardene, for example, whose purposes are low and dark and slimy. I've no fear of speaking so about the man, for he well knows how I feel about him. And I've no stomach for him and his kind and neither has Gil Paxton."

Con Waters had been speaking with his head slightly bent and his eyes fixed on a corner of the shadowed room. Now he straightened and his glance struck Allard squarely.

"If it should happen, Mister Allard, that you came up wearing the badge of night marshal, would you be willing to stand foursquare on the principle of making our town of Pawnee a better town, or would your only concern be the working out of your own vengeance?"

Allard turned and stared hard at Gil Paxton, who spoke quietly.

"Believe I told you, Allard, that Con here heard the shot that killed Jim Creightly, and that he helped me carry Creightly into my store. Con was right at my side when Creightly told me to get in touch with you. So he knows the main reason you want the job of night marshal. We three, along with Doc Sanchez, are the only ones who know the story, and you can bet on Doc. He'll never utter a word. For he's another of us who liked the way Pawnee was before Pinto Jardene and others of his kind showed up."

Allard nodded curtly and turned back to Con Waters. "You got a marshal here—that fellow Mosby. What's holding him back?"

"Jardene's man," snapped Waters. "Oh, not openly or even consciously, perhaps. There have been times when I thought I glimpsed quite a show of good fiber in Lee Mosby. But there is also a streak of the cynical politician in the man and he inclines as he does because he figures it good politics. He rides on what he figures to be the high tide of opinion, and he sees that opinion in Pinto Jardene and Haley Twitchell. So he tends to making excuses instead of acting, if he figures the acting would meet with the approval of Jardene and Twitchell."

"When I hit town this afternoon I saw a dead man in the back of a spring wagon," Allard said. "That an example of what you mean?"

"A perfect one," put in Gil Paxton. "Flick Lester, a Bench cowhand, was one of Barbara Chancellor's riders. He ran into a crooked, off the bottom-of-the-deck deal in the Palace and was killed when he objected.

Mosby claims that witnesses to the affair swear that Lester went for his gun first—and perhaps he did. The big point is, however, that if the deal had been fair, Lester wouldn't have gone for his gun at all. He'd have taken his loss and let it go at that. For I knew Flick Lester well, and he was a good sport and not at all the sort to start trouble without a good cause. There have been other cases somewhat similar."

"Should I get on as night man, this fellow Mosby would be giving me orders," Allard pointed out. "And if I went against those orders he'd give me the boot."

"Now there you're wrong," assured Con Waters quickly. "Once he accepts you and you take over the job, Mosby can't get rid of you with just a wave of his hand. He'd have to convince Gil and me, which would be anything but easy."

"If Mosby isn't a satisfactory marshal, why haven't you fired him a long time ago?" Allard demanded bluntly.

"Now that is a fair question," acknowledged Waters slowly. "And something we've considered, too. But in the first place, we'd have to make a fight of it with Jardene and Twitchell and maybe we wouldn't be quite strong enough to win. Again, who would we put in Mosby's place? Even with such as Mosby for marshal is better than no marshal at all. So you see, Mister Allard, there are wheels within wheels as the saying goes. However, once we could get our kind of man in as night marshal, we've a big point to stand on. But he must be our kind of man."

"And you feel that maybe I am?"

"That," said Con Waters, "is for you to answer, Mister Allard."

Allard's cigar had gone out. He touched a match to the stove and when it burst into flame, brought his cigar to a glow once more. He considered the picture soberly, and saw with perfect clarity what he'd be stepping into. This town of Pawnee was obviously divided, the sound and decent element on one side, the off-color element on the other. And he would be walking the dubious path that ran between these two sides. It was hardly a promising prospect.

"It could," he murmured, speaking his thought aloud, a sardonic note in his words, "turn out to be a damn lonely spot."

"Aye," nodded Con Waters, quick to understand. "Lonely, and dangerous, too. It wouldn't be fair to represent it to you as otherwise. The choice is yours."

Allard became abruptly harsh. "With the chips really down, how much backing could I depend on? Once I took a stand on what I figured as right, I'd expect backing. Would I get it or would I be fed to the wolves?"

"You'd get backing," said Waters crisply. "You ride on the side of common decency and decency will ride with you, all the way! Give us honest performance and you'll have no worries there. But your tone just now is wrong, Mister Allard. Remember, it was you who asked us for the job, not the other way around."

"Sorry," said Allard gruffly. "Didn't mean it that way. I'm just trying to get all the picture." He stared at the ash on the tip of his cigar then brushed it off with a flick of his finger. "I might have to get tough, damned tough."

"No might about it," agreed Waters. "You'll have to. If a situation demands toughness, show it—show just as much as is necessary. We'll still ride with you."

"Very well," said Allard. "If you're satisfied, I am."

A quick, small smile touched Con Waters' lips and his hand came out. "Friend, I think we understand each other. From what I'd seen of Jim Creightly, I liked him. So I wish you success in your quest there. Beyond that, if you'll put a little steel into the running of this town, why then it's a bargain to the benefit of all of us."

Con Waters turned to Gil Paxton. "It'll be your chore, Gil, to sell this man Allard to Pinto Jardene and Haley

Twitchell. You've a smoother tongue and way with those men than I have."

Town Marshal Lee Mosby's office was made up of two rooms at the corner of a building standing midway along the run of the street, the rear room being where he lodged. When Frank Allard and Gil Paxton came in, Mosby was seated at his desk, a fair-haired man with a bleached mustache who carried enough surplus flesh to show the start of jowls on his somewhat heavy-featured face. He looked up and grunted a brief greeting.

"Damned raw outside, Gil."

"All of that," nodded Paxton. "Lee, shake hands with Frank Allard. How does he shape up to you as a night man?"

Mosby straightened in his chair, his glance going sharp as he looked Allard up and down. "Big enough. Where'd you pick him up?"

"He just rode in and hit me up for the job. Asked if there was an opening for that kind of work and I told him there might be."

Mosby's handshake was brief. He eyed Allard with a certain frowning wariness. "Sounds too simple, Gil. Must be more to it than that."

"There is," explained Allard. "I was at the store this afternoon and happened to overhear the talk between you and Paxton after that girl had driven away with a dead man in her wagon. I heard you say you could use a night man. So..." He shrugged.

Mosby settled back in his chair, still studying Allard. "I need a night man, all right," he conceded. "You had any experience in that line of work?"

"None to speak of. But I learn pretty fast."

Mosby still showed a calculating hesitancy, so Gil Paxton spoke bluntly.

"Lee, you've been crying for a night man. Now either you need one or you don't. If you do, here I think is a good one. If you don't, then I don't want to hear you crying about being overworked anymore. So—what's it to be?"

There was a bite in Paxton's words that brought a slight flush to Mosby's heavy face. "Give a man time to think, can't you?" he blurted. "You don't buy a horse the first minute you lay eyes on it." Again that air of hesitation before Mosby shrugged. "All right. You know damn well that I need a night man, and right now I'd settle for a lot less than this fellow. But Pinto will want to have a look at him."

"So, I imagine," said Paxton, "will Haley Twitchell. They'll probably be at their regular game?"

"I expect," growled Mosby. "We'll go see."

He stood up, donned his canvas coat, blew out the lamp, and led the way into the street. Now the wind as well as the rain had dwindled out, and the night was thick with a sodden dankness that lifted from the puddled earth and bit at a man's bones. Mosby hurried his lunging stride toward the Palace.

Here was gaudiness to go with the name. A long bar, close-packed gambling tables, and a cleared area at the far end where several flounced dance-hall girls lounged minus partners, and where a slender, black-haired, thin-faced man with strangely pallid skin idled at a piano.

Mosby jerked a nod to a bartender. "Business slow, eh Chet?"

"Dead as hell," was the flat rejoinder. "Might as well close up for the night. What's on your mind?"

"Pinto," said Mosby.

"Out back. Him and the two Twitchells. Ned Fargo and Harry Shelline."

Mosby went to a rear door, knocked, then opened it, and led the way through without waiting for a summons. Five men were at a poker table under the circular cone of radiance flooding down from an overhead lamp. Mosby directed his words at one of the players, a touch of apology in his manner.

"Sorry to bother, Pinto, but this won't take long. Gil Paxton has dug up a night man for me, and I wanted you to have a look at him. If he suits you, he suits me."

Gil Paxton took a step to the front. "This is Frank Allard, gentlemen. As you probably recall, we've been promising Mosby a night man for some time, and Allard is willing to consider the job. And Allard, starting from here and around the table it's Royce Twitchell, the son, then Harry Shelline, Haley Twitchell, the father, Ned Fargo, and Pinto Jardene."

Allard had his quick, measuring glance at them. Royce Twitchell was a stocky, curly-haired young fellow, good-looking in a florid way, but with a somewhat spoiled, sarcastic-looking mouth and eyes that carried a hot restlessness in their depths. Harry Shelline was plainly all tinhorn gambler, a neutral-looking sort, without a shade of expression on his pale, locked features.

Like his son, Haley Twitchell was stocky. He was red-faced, bald. He chewed wetly on the remains of a tattered cigar, the juice of which laid its brown stain at the corners of his mouth and along the edges of his heavy lips. Ned Fargo was a riding man, with the smell of horse sweat on him. His face was bony and hard and under jutting brows his eyes seemed to have receded to a cold wariness. He badly needed a shave and lank hair hung raggedly about his shirt collar.

It was Pinto Jardene who was the dominating figure at the table. At that moment he pushed his chair back, got to his feet, and moved over to a chair that had a black, broadcloth coat hung across it. The Palace owner dredged a cigar from a pocket of the garment and while he nipped off the end of the perfecto, lighted it, and rolled it between his lips, he studied Frank Allard with small, hard, heavily lidded eyes.

A man of average size, this Pinto Jardene owned to a certain sleek plumpness. His smooth-shaven face was unlined and on the swarthy side. His lips were full, sensuous. His hair was sleek and coal-black except for a streak of almost silver-gray which ran along the left side of his head. The contrast of this was startling, marking the man as definitely as a physical disfigurement might have, and was obviously the source of the nickname Pinto. He moved with an unhurried, but soft efficiency that carried a suggestion of the feline about it. In Frank Allard's eyes, this Pinto Jardene was, on first survey, a dangerous man.

It was Royce Twitchell who spoke first. "Your regular trade, Allard—packing a badge?"

"No. But if I felt I couldn't handle the job I wouldn't have asked for it."

"Maybe," went on young Twitchell, "you're one of the breed who fancies himself with a gun—and is always looking for an excuse to use it?" There was a caustic bite in both tone and words.

Frost edged Allard's eyes. This young buck had a way with him that got under a man's skin. Allard held onto his temper, though his answer was curt.

"I can use a gun if I have to, but using it is not my trade, if that's what you're driving at."

"Just what is your trade—saddle-bum?"

This brought a raw harshness leaping out of Allard. "Whatever it might be, it's not taking any whipsawing from such as you. What makes you so proud?"

Now it was the elder Twitchell who spoke up quickly. "Just a minute, Allard—let it lay, let it lay! And Royce, you keep that damned sarcastic tongue of yours to yourself. Quit trying to throw your weight around. Now I, for one, like this man Allard's style. And Gil you must like it, too, or you wouldn't be recommending him. Pinto, what's your opinion?"

Whatever it was, Pinto Jardene was not expanding on it to any great length. He shrugged his sleek shoulders with a callous indifference, giving off the impression that this whole thing was more or less boring to him. When he finally answered, his voice was purring and smooth as his face.

"Suits you, suits me. Anything to keep Mosby from crying around how badly he's overworked. We can," he added, with a certain soft ruthlessness, "always get rid of this fellow Allard if he doesn't suit us."

"Well then," said the elder Twitchell, "I guess we can call the matter settled."

"If it is," snapped Royce Twitchell, "let's get on with the game."

Lee Mosby, feeling that this shut them out, jerked his head toward the door and led the way. As they emerged into the big barroom Gil Paxton dropped a hand on Frank Allard's arm, murmuring—"Good luck!"

Allard showed him a small smile. "Thanks, I may need it. How come they don't invite you into that game?"

Paxton's answering smile was dry, a little wintry. "I'm not interested and they know it. Oh, I can enjoy a friendly game of draw for low stakes where nobody gets hurt, win or lose. But those fellows don't play that type of game. Besides, I've a business to take care of. Right now I've some books to work over before I can turn in."

Outside, Paxton headed for his store, while Frank Allard and Lee Mosby stopped at Mosby's office, where the marshal got the lamp going again. He waved Allard to a chair, took the one behind the desk, and settled into it with a grunting sigh.

"Sometimes I wonder why any man is damn fool enough to pack a badge," he growled. "It's a dog's life. No matter what you do or don't do, you're wrong. Whichever way you move you're stepping on the toes of somebody who sets up a yell. You're between hell and high water all the time."

"Then," drawled Allard, "why not do what you figure is right and let the chips fall, regardless?"

Mosby shrugged. "Sounds fine, but it ain't that simple or easy."

"Yet you hang onto the job."

"That's right, I do," agreed the marshal. "But I'm not riding law on this town because I yearn to bring sweetness and light to a lot of damn fools who wouldn't recognize such things if hit square in the face with them. This is just a job to me, a way to earn a living. And bad as it is, I prefer it to punching cattle. Better pay for one thing. Also, I eat better and sleep in a bed with a roof over my head, in good weather or bad. Which beats all hell out of crawling in and out of a wet soogan along a rainy trail somewhere, as I've done plenty often in my time."

Mosby dug around in the desk drawer, came up with a pipe which he packed, and carefully lighted. Then, through a drift of smoke, he looked at Allard with shrewd intentness.

"It'll pay you to get the picture straight, Allard. There'll be times when you got to play both ends against the middle. It's like this. If I want to keep this job, which I do, then there's certain people I got to play along with. Like Pinto Jardene, for instance. Make no mistake about it, but when you get all through measuring them, Pinto's the big man in this town. He packs the real weight. Next to him comes Haley Twitchell. He runs the bank, which means that he's got the wallop of money behind him. He and Pinto play their cards pretty much alike, and it's them two we got to please."

"What about young Twitchell?" asked Allard. "What does he rate? For I'm afraid I'm liable to have words with that fellow if I'm around him too much."

Mosby waved a soothing hand. "He's just a spoiled, conceited pup. As you've seen, there's a mean, sarcastic streak in him. But when his old man snaps the whip, young Royce jumps into line. Funny way the old man has with him. In some ways he's soft as mush, in others tough as hell. I can't ever remember Royce doing a lick

33

of work. Oh, he's supposed to be a vice-president or something of the sort in the old man's bank, but everybody knows it doesn't mean a damn thing. His main activity, so it seems, is paying court to that Chancellor girl. If he could make a match of it there and so get a hold of the big C Cross ranch up on the Bench, and with his old man's money behind him, I guess he figures he'd be set for life. I've heard it said that Royce's interest in Barbara Chancellor is one activity of his that the old man approves of thoroughly."

Frank Allard, remembering a slim, slicker-swathed girl about to face a long drive through the murk and rain with a dead man in the back of her spring wagon, stirred a little restlessly. "Paxton," he offered, "strikes me as being pretty regular."

"Oh, sure," agreed Mosby. "Gil's all right. He's what I'd call a plain, honest, decent man. But Gil's big trouble is that he can't get away from dreaming about what he calls the good old days, before the railroad came through and the trail outfits began driving in to put some life in the town. So he keeps yelping for what he calls law and order. Part of that is, I suppose, due to the fact that he never will get over being bitter about his wife. He blames that on the railroad and the town's new setup, I suppose."

Allard swung his head. "How's that?"

Mosby hesitated slightly, then shrugged. "You'd hear about it sooner or later, anyhow. Seems she was considerably younger than Gil, and high-spirited, so I understand. And when the railroad sent an engineering crew through here to survey for the line, there was a transit man that Gil's wife was kind of taken with. She ran off with him."

"Thing like that would sour any man," said Allard. Then, changing the subject—"That gambler, Shelline—he didn't seem to be worrying any over having killed a man today."

Mosby shifted in his chair. "Cold-blooded as a snake,

Shelline is. But the killing was one of those things. Cowhand tried to buck the tiger, lost his money, and wanted to shoot somebody. Hell, man! You've been around. You know there's a damn lot more sinners than saints in the world. You ever hear of a trail-town that was skim-milk mild? No, and you never will."

Mosby paused to run another match across the bowl of his pipe. "You take men fresh in off a tough drive trail, or cowhands in town with a month's wages burning holes in their pockets—you take such and mix them with liquor and cards and dance-hall girls, and you're bound to come up with a hat-ful of trouble. All any man with a badge can do is keep things from getting completely out of hand. When you ready to go on duty?"

"Right now, if you want it that way."

"Fair enough." Mosby rummaged through the desk drawer again and came up with a badge tarnished with age and disuse. He tossed this across to Allard. "Put that on and you're it. No need of going through all that foolishness of taking an oath. This is just another job, and you're hired. You'll draw a hundred and twenty-five a month. We'll work out the shift hours to make it easiest on both of us. Tonight we'll both be able to get some sleep, as things are pretty quiet. The last trail herd shipped out four days ago. I understand there are a couple more on their way in, but there's no telling when they'll arrive. Probably be a couple or three days. And the storm has kept most of the Bench riders undercover. If you'd like, before you turn in, I'll take you over the beat and show you what things look like."

"Sounds like a good idea," Allard said, nodding.

As they went out again and along the street, a lank figure emerged from the Palace, moved to a horse at the hitch rail, and went slogging off into the night out the western end of the street.

"Ned Fargo," identified Mosby. "Tough chunk, that fellow, from what I've heard. But he's never caused me any fuss in this town. Friend of Pinto Jardene. They come and they go, Allard, the tough ones and the weak ones, the good ones and the bad. World will always be that way, I guess. Long as they leave me alone, it's all right with me."

An hour later, Frank Allard was back in his room in the hotel. He got the lamp going, took off his coat, and lit a cigar. For some time he lounged at ease on the bed, lost in thought. Finally he sat up, unpinned the badge on his shirt, and studied it. Then, in abrupt decision he opened his warbag, brought out the oily cloth that had been wrapped around his gun, and set to work cleaning and polishing the badge. He worked until all sign of tarnish was gone and the metal shone brightly. Then he pinned it back on his shirt.

He blew out the lamp, then stood at his window while finishing his cigar. Below him the street was a dark gulf, with a few lights strung feebly along its edges. A quiet night, Lee Mosby had called it—one of the few.

A quirk of Allard's thoughts likened the town to a jungle animal resting now, and satiated, because that day it had killed its man. A rider named Flick Lester, who had gone back to his home ranch, lying dead under a soggy tarpaulin, while the rain beat down, and the wind droned its mournful dirge.

Yeah, a dead man going home in the back of a spring wagon, a wagon driven by a slender girl in a yellow slicker. A girl of courage, as Gil Paxton had said, and one who by her own words had come to hate the town and all that it held.

In recollection he saw her again as she stood for those few moments on the porch of Gil Paxton's store, while adjusting the throat latch of her hat, saw too the strain of grief and revulsion on her face, and heard her voice running flat and toneless and gray, because of so much bottled-up emotion.

Allard thought of other things, of Jim Creightly, a partner who rode away and never came back. Because this town had killed him, too. This town of Pawnee,

36

with its dives and its deadfalls, with its vultures and harpies. This—as Gil Paxton had called it—this goddamned town!

Allard stirred, a hand going up to touch the newly polished badge on his shirt. There was, so Lee Mosby had said when giving over that badge, no need of going through the foolishness of taking an oath. For this was just another job, a way of earning a living. And to hold that job you'd have to walk softly around Pinto Jardene and others of his ilk. Pinto Jardene, the big man of the town.

Frank Allard's lip curled a trifle. He tossed the dead butt of his cigar out the window, undressed, turned in, and was swiftly asleep.

CHAPTER THREE

IT WAS AS fine a morning as a man could ask for. The full weather change had come sometime during the small hours of the morning. Lowering clouds had drifted and cleared and now, with a brilliant sun glinting across the world, the sky was a deep-washed blue and everything seemed to shine from the cleansing of the rain. As the touch of the sun grew in power the world steamed and smoked with mists that lifted and dissolved. There was a briskness in the air to sting a man's lungs and send the good tide of life flowing vigorously.

Frank Allard, savoring his after-breakfast cigar, headed along the street to the livery barn, where Con Waters stood out front, welcoming the touch of the sun.

The livery owner showed a small contained smile and a grave turn of his head.

"Now if I was a superstitious man," he murmured, "I might see it all as a sign. A bright and shining day and a bright and shining badge of office. It looks good on you, friend."

"There's more weight to it than I thought there'd be," Allard answered. "I didn't realize that fully until I'd pinned it on."

Con Waters ducked his head again. "Now that proves that Gil Paxton and I were right in our judgment of you. You're a man of conscience, and to such a man a badge of office is ever a weighty thing. It represents so much more than the casual eye might see. Gil tells me that you've met the high and the low. What do you think of them?"

Allard considered gravely. "I never give my full judgment on a horse until I've ridden it. In this case I haven't as yet stepped into the saddle."

There sounded the mutter of hoofs on wet earth and a rider cut into the street from a road that led down from the Bench country to the north. Allard started slightly. The rider was the girl of the afternoon before.

She was not wearing the yellow slicker now, but instead a snugly buttoned buckskin jacket which emphasized the straightness of her shoulders and the full lithe vigor of her. The ends of a white silk neckerchief fluttered at her throat.

"Barbara Chancellor!" exclaimed Con Waters softly. "Now what would she be wanting back in this town today? After the happenings of yesterday and the things she said to Gil Paxton, a man might think she'd never want to see the town again."

Allard said nothing, watching the girl. She headed directly to Gil Paxton's store, swung down, and ran in. Haste was in her every move, in the blowing and hard-ridden condition of her horse.

It was only a moment or two before both she and Gil

Paxton came out of the store. From the edge of the porch Paxton looked up and down the street, then across to where Allard and Con Waters stood. He lifted an arm and beckoned.

"Now it's one or both of us that Gil wants," said Waters. "Let's get over there."

They went across and it was to Allard that Paxton spoke. "Could be a mite of trouble heading this way, Frank. Barbara's crew is riding in after Harry Shelline. She wants them headed off. I don't know just where Lee Mosby is right now, so it seems it's up to you."

Allard looked at the girl. She was watching him with clear, grave eyes that were shadowed with worry. "You mean," he asked, "that this crew of yours is riding against your orders?"

"Yes." Her voice was low and taut. "When I got home last night with Flick Lester, they were wild with anger. This morning my foreman, Lafe Oglevie, told me what they intended to do. I tried to argue but it did no good. So as soon as they were out of sight of the ranch I caught up a horse and rode to beat them here. I used some short cuts, but they should be showing any minute."

"They said what they intended to do with this gambler—this Harry Shelline?"

She nodded, and her tone grew in intensity. "One of them has a special rope, already noosed, hanging on his saddle horn. They made it out of Flick Lester's riata. Maybe Shelline deserves to be lynched, but I don't want my crew mixed up in any such affair. For they are a good crew. I know their worth, even though they now intend to go past my orders. I can understand why they feel as they do, but I—I want them stopped."

"How many of them?" Allard asked.

"Six."

Allard's eyes pinched down. "Could turn out to be pretty rough. I'll rustle up Mosby and we'll do our best." He turned to hurry off, and the girl's call followed him.

41

"There must be no gunplay."

Allard did not answer, but his thought was that this thing might be anything but a simple chore. For six angry, vengeance-bound men could hardly be held back by the wave of a hand.

He had no idea where Mosby might be, as he hadn't seen the man since parting with him last night. First chance would be the office, but this chance was as empty as the office proved to be. Allard swung rapidly along to the Palace.

The barroom was garishly empty, except for a lone bartender and a swamper, the latter swinging a listless broom. Allard caught the bartender's eye. "Seen Lee Mosby anywhere around?"

A nod indicated the back room. "In there."

Allard moved to the rear door, opened it, and stepped through. Mosby was there, all right. So was Pinto Jardene, and the gambler, Harry Shelline. Pinto Jardene was in the midst of a harsh remark. He hesitated only briefly at Allard's abrupt entrance, then went on to finish what he was saying.

"Get this, Mosby—and get it right! No part of your job is to try and tell me how to run my affairs. Harry Shelline is one of my boys, and I take care of those who work for me. That's final!"

Under the bite of Jardene's tone, Lee Mosby's face was flushed and his eyes were sulky. He turned to Allard with relief. "Looking for me?"

"That's right," Allard said. "Little chore ahead. I understand there's half a dozen mad cowboys on their way into town, packing a noosed rope. They're looking for a tinhorn by the name of Shelline. Bunkies of a rider named Lester, they are."

Allard was watching Shelline as he spoke, and he saw the gambler's pallid jaw tighten and a glint of uneasiness brush his cold eyes.

Mosby was startled. "You mean the C Cross crew are coming after Shelline?"

"How it shapes up," Allard nodded.

"Who brought the word?"

"Owner of the spread—Miss Chancellor."

"What the hell!" Mosby blurted. "They're her crew. Why don't she stop them herself?"

Impatience put a rasp into Frank Allard's voice. "Men full of rightful hate have been known to go against orders of their boss before this. Anyway, while the lady admits that maybe the tinhorn deserves to be strung up, she doesn't want her crew to take on the chore. We're wasting time, here. Let's get outside."

Lee Mosby turned to Pinto Jardene with a smug smile of triumph. "So it looks like I was right all the time, Pinto."

Jardene took out a cigar and lit it with steady hands. "All I see in this is a chance for you to strut your badge, Mosby. Strut it and make it stick. Get on out there. Stop that crowd at the limits of town and take their guns away from them. Call that a new ordinance adopted just for today. No riders allowed in town with a gun." He smiled cynically past the smoke of his cigar.

Mosby turned to leave and Allard followed him, then brought up short as Jardene's next words hit directly at him.

"You—Allard! A few words of advice to you. I don't like the way you keep referring to a man of mine as a tinhorn. And the next time you come into this room you knock first and then you wait for a summons before you come in. Is that straight enough for you? Don't get too proud over the badge you're wearing. It's only tin."

Allard came fully around, eyeing this sleek, dark man with a coldly measuring intentness. His reply ran curt. "To me a tinhorn gambler is always a tinhorn. And you're wrong about the badge. No tin in it, just good, honest metal. And I'll take it into any room where it needs to be taken without asking permission from you or anybody else, Jardene. Maybe you figure yourself as the big man on the top of the hill. I don't see you as such!"

He turned on his heel and walked out.

In the street, Lee Mosby headed along at his lunging walk. As Allard moved up even with him, Mosby spoke without turning his head.

"Apparently your new job don't mean much to you. Good thing it don't, for you won't be keeping it long, talking to Pinto the way you did."

Allard's reply was cold. "Any time that Pinto Jardene thinks he can reach high enough to take this badge off me, let him step up and try. That could go for others, too."

Mosby flashed him a quick and startled glance, but said nothing more on the subject.

The girl, Barbara Chancellor, stood waiting at the store steps with Gil Paxton and Con Waters. Coming up to them, Mosby spoke with a hint of annoyed roughness.

"What's the matter with that crew of yours, Miss Chancellor? Doesn't an order from their boss mean anything to them? What kind of men have you got riding for you, anyhow?"

The girl flushed and her chin came up. "They're good men, all of them. They wouldn't be riding for me if they weren't. And though they are wrong in this, I can certainly understand their anger. Flick Lester's death might mean nothing to you, but it does to them."

Con Waters, who had been watching the lift of the Bench road above town, spoke with a soft dryness.

"If you got any ideas, Mosby—you better put them to work. Because here they come!"

The Bench road was a swift-dropping tangent across the slope of country north of town. And out there now, riding at a measured lope, a compact group of riders showed. Lee Mosby stared, his heavy face pulled into a scowl.

"Them who howl loudest for law and order are the

first to jump over the traces. Just what do those fools figure they're going to do?"

"Believe I told you about that in the Palace," said Allard. "They're packing a special rope for Shelline. Either way, our chore is to do something first. Come on!"

He headed for the junction of the road and the street. With him he carried a picture of Barbara Chancellor's paling, worried face. Behind him he could hear Lee Mosby's heavy step and the growling mumble of the man's uneasy anger. Mosby, he decided, was showing signs of being anything but a staunch pillar to lean on.

At the junction Allard stopped and watched the approach of the group of riders with shadowed eyes. Lee Mosby came up beside him, complaining.

"Six of them—two of us. If they really mean business, what can we do about it? Far as I'm concerned they can have Shelline. When you found me in the Palace I'd been trying to convince Pinto Jardene that it might be smart if Shelline dropped out of sight for a while. He wouldn't listen. So now—why should we worry any about Shelline's hide?"

Allard flashed him a quick look, then glanced away again, a gorge of contempt rising in his throat. "You miss the point, Mosby. There's either law in this town or there's not. You pack a badge. Well then, make it mean what it stands for!"

The riders came on, with a hint of the ominous in the steadiness of their approach. Riding a little in front was a man who made a big, solid figure in the saddle.

"If you figure to stop them," spurred Allard, "now's the time to do it."

Mosby cursed sullenly, stepped out, and threw up a hand. The riding group slowed from a lope to a trot, then to a walk, and finally to a halt, the big man in the lead reining in but a couple of paces from Mosby. A voice as big as its owner rumbled in deep resonance.

"Feeling proud this morning, Mosby?"

Mosby flushed. "Just curious, Oglevie. Wondering just where you aim to go and what you aim to do when you get there?"

"You know damn well where we aim to go and what we aim to do or you wouldn't be out here, trying to run a bluff," was the curt reply. "Had a hunch Barbara would short-cut into town ahead of us."

Lee Mosby seemed to gather a little confidence. "What sort of a crew are you? Doesn't an order from your boss mean anything to you? Or is it because the boss is a young woman that you figure to do as you please?"

"That," said the big man quietly, "is entirely between Barbara and us—and none of your business, Mosby."

One of the other riders spoke up impatiently. "We're wasting time, Lafe. Move that cheap sketch of a marshal out of the way and let's get on about our little chore."

Over his shoulder, Lafe Oglevie growled. "Don't push on the reins, Lark!" He fixed a stern glance fully on Mosby again. "It's like this, Mosby. Me and the boys, we came into town to clean up a little business that's been pressing to be done for a long time. When we're through with that business the air will be a lot cleaner. We don't want to start a general hassle, but if we have to we'll tear this damn town apart to get our little chore done. Now you be smart. Get out of the way and stay there, and in half an hour we'll have finished what we came for and be on our way home. You can make it hard or easy for yourself. Well?"

Allard, silent, watching and listening, missed no word or shade of expression. Now, in Mosby, he saw bluff turn to indecision and indecision to defeat. Lafe Oglevie saw this, too, and he lifted his reins.

"That's being smart, Mosby. You just find yourself a nice quiet spot and stay there out of the way for about half an hour."

Lee Mosby shuffled to one side, eyes averted, face suffused with a sullen shame. And right here, thought Frank Allard, was full proof of something Mosby had said to him last night. Packing the town marshal badge in this town of Pawnee was just a job to Lee Mosby— just a job and nothing more. To that job the man brought neither pride or any fundamental sense of integrity. A front, apparently, was all Lee Mosby owned— a false front with only sawdust behind it.

Yet, despite all this, Mosby represented something which he, Frank Allard also represented—something which these C Cross men had no right to override or scorn. Allard's eyes began to frost up and the current of cold purpose ran through him.

Lafe Oglevie was stirring his horse to movement again when Allard's voice hit him.

"Just a minute!"

With the words, Allard moved out into the middle of the road and street junction, his voice harsh. "Lee's not alone. There's two of us. And this thing stops right here!"

Lafe Oglevie pulled up again, staring in some surprise. His curt demand rumbled. "Now then, just who in hell are you?"

"Allard's the name—Frank Allard. But that part doesn't matter. What counts is this." He touched the badge on his shirt. "Night marshal is the official title, I suppose. Yet I can work in the daytime, too—like now, when Lee's hand needs backing. I suggest we talk things over."

They measured each other, the big man in the saddle, the rangy raw-boned man who stood afoot, holding down the center of the road junction. The grizzle of middle age had frosted Lafe Oglevie's temples. There was a weathered look to his solid jawed face, product of a lifetime in the open. It wasn't a wild, unruly face, decided Allard, but instead one that was full of strength and character. This man was solid—worthwhile.

Somehow, too, there was a lionlike quality about Lafe Oglevie, heightened by the golden brown color of his eyes and by the heavy mane of hair showing beneath his tipped back hat. His eyes puckered at the corners in a way that suggested sternness, but also the saving grace of a broad and understanding humor. Here, thought Frank Allard, was a man he could instinctively like, even though right now a wall of will lifted between the two of them.

"All right," rumbled Oglevie. "So you're something new that's been added to this damn town. And I can see a different color in you than in Mosby. But that's not changing the facts. You know why the boys and me are here?"

Allard nodded. "I know. And it won't do."

The impatient rider sounded off again. "Just another of Pinto Jardene's pet poodles, Lafe. Ride him down!"

Allard's glance sought out the speaker, a thin, dark intense-looking cowhand. "You're wrong both ways, friend. Not any pet poodle of Jardene's, and I don't ride down easy. So let's keep the top on this thing and see if we can hit a point of understanding."

Lafe Oglevie leaned forward in his saddle, crossed his forearms on his saddle horn. "All right," he said abruptly. "I'm willing to spare a minute for listening."

Allard picked his words with slow care. "That gun showdown between Flick Lester and the tinhorn, Shelline—do you know all the facts of it?"

"Know enough, and all that's necessary," rumbled Oglevie. "That fellow Shelline killed a C Cross rider. Flick Lester was a good man, while Shelline is just what you called him, a damn, cheap, bottom-of-the-deck tinhorn. And if you're not a Jardene man, why are you taking Shelline's part?"

"I'm not taking Shelline's part," Allard differed. "The point I'm driving at, is that so far I've seen no proof that the gunplay wasn't an even break. As I know the account, it is that Lester sat in a game, lost his stack, then went for his gun. And Shelline shot in self-defense. That could be the truth, or it could be a lie. So, until we find out...!"

The intense, impatient rider suddenly dug the spurs into his horse. "Talk—talk!" he snarled. "I'm fed up with it!"

He came surging past Lafe Oglevie, straight at Allard, who slid a quick stride to the side, reaching out and up to lock a hand in the rider's belt and put the weight of his shoulders into a powerful, whirling drag that brought the rider, Lark, lunging out of his saddle. Allard used the weight of the man's fall to give him a swinging throw. Lark, rolling, smashed into the side of a building, and huddled there, dazed and half-stunned.

Allard, slightly crouched, was set to lash out at the rest of the group, but Lafe Oglevie got there first, his deep voice an angry roar.

"Steady, everybody! Lark asked for that. Steady! I'll handle this!"

The other riders, who had started forward in concerted anger, slowed, and Lafe Oglevie rapped out another order.

"Casey, get over there and take care of Lark's gun before he makes a bigger fool of himself. Hurry up!"

The rider, Casey, was quickly down and over to Lark, grabbing the latter's gun just ahead of Lark's fumbling hand. Lark lifted to his knees, then his feet, his back, and hands propped against the wall behind him. He'd lost his hat and his dark hair hung over his bitter eyes. He seemed ready to come at Allard again, but Lafe Oglevie's growl clubbed him back.

"Right there, Lark—stay right there! You jump the gun on me again and you draw your time. You hear me!"

It had been a close thing, an abrupt eruption of violence that could have turned into something deadly. Now it was done with, and the moment of savage danger had passed, brought so by the dominant personality of this big man, Lafe Oglevie. Straightening from his crouch, Allard looked at Oglevie with deepening respect.

"Thanks," he said evenly. "You're all decent men and I want no trouble with any of you, but while I wear this badge, it's going to mean what it stands for. Don't think I'm condoning the killing of Flick Lester, because I'm not. On the other hand, self-defense is self-defense, even for a tinhorn. However," and here Allard's glance moved from man to man of the C Cross crew, "the weight of evidence suggests that Harry Shelline is an undesirable character, one the town could be much better off without. So—Harry Shelline is leaving Pawnee. He gets a floater...He'll be out of town by sundown. That's a promise."

"I'll have to see that," rapped a rider skeptically. "The tinhorn is one of Jardene's pets, and Jardene runs this town."

"And I suppose," sneered Lark, "that running Shelline out of town will make Flick Lester rest easier?"

Lafe Oglevie waved them to silence, his eyes fixedly on Allard. "You mean that? You'll run Shelline out of town? You think you can make that stick?"

"I mean it. And I'll make it stick."

Oglevie ruminated for a moment in silence. Then he jerked his head in decision.

"Good enough. I'll meet any man halfway. But I'll be back in town tomorrow, Allard, to see with my own eyes. If you've made good—fine! But if you haven't, why then me and the boys will finish the job we came on today. And should you try and stop us, it'll be your funeral. That's it!"

Lafe Oglevie reined his horse half-around. "All right, there Lark. Back in your saddle! We're pulling out."

They didn't want to go. The purpose that had brought them to Pawnee, still burned in them hotly. But they couldn't push their anger past Lafe Oglevie. One of them rounded up Lark's horse for him. Lark had recovered his hat and he beat this into shape before swinging into his saddle. He gave Frank Allard another hot and angry glance, then dropped in with the others and followed Lafe Oglevie out of town.

Allard watched them until the swing of the road's climbing slope put them out of sight. After that he turned back to face the town.

Lee Mosby was fifty yards away, heading for the office. Down at the doors of the Palace the dapper figure of Harry Shelline stood motionless—motionless until Frank Allard's searching glance touched him. Then he slipped through the doors and out of sight. Over on the porch of the store Gil Paxton and Barbara Chancellor and Con Waters stood waiting. Allard went slowly over to them. It was Con Waters who spoke.

"We could see, but we couldn't hear it all. I know Lafe Oglevie and he doesn't scare easy. Just what was it you said or did to calm matters down, man?"

"I promised Oglevie I'd run Shelline out of town," Allard said.

Gil Paxton exclaimed. "That means you're throwing the glove squarely into the face of more than Shelline!"

"What you wanted, wasn't it?" rapped Allard curtly. Then in a milder tone he added, "It was the only way to head off something that could have worked out pretty mean and dirty."

He looked at Barbara Chancellor. She was watching him, and now there was relief in her gray eyes. Her face and throat were softly tanned, and morning's sunlight did things to her skin, giving it a sort of golden glow. Now that the strain of anxiety had left her, her mouth had softened into curves of an inherent sweetness. This girl, thought Allard, in a gay and laughing mood would flash with real beauty. He smiled gravely.

"I like that foreman of yours, Miss Chancellor. I hope you won't spur him too hard for going past your orders."

She showed him a small answering smile. "How

could I? Lafe Oglevie is like a second father to me. As for the rest of this unfortunate affair—thank you!"

Allard touched his hat and headed for the office, bracing himself mentally for the fireworks he knew would be waiting there. For Lee Mosby would have plenty of such cooked up for him. Mosby had been shamed and, after Lafe Oglevie's first harsh pronouncements, virtually ignored by all parties. So, unless the man was a complete sluggard, he was bound to be in a savage state of mind.

No matter, thought Allard bleakly, what had to be, would be. A man could only play the part the Fates allotted to him...

Watching after Allard, Con Waters cleared his throat and made a soft pronouncement. "There's a man come to our town, Gil Paxton. Yonder he goes...!"

CHAPTER FOUR

LEE MOSBY was sitting at his desk, hunched forward, shoulders slumped, his eyes and face heavy with a dark surliness. Without looking at Frank Allard he growled, "Take it off!"

"Take what off?" asked Allard.

"You know damn well what I mean. That badge. Take it off. You're through!"

Allard lowered himself into a chair and while he built and lighted a cigarette, let the straining silence build and build. When he finally spoke, it was quietly. "No. I'm not taking the badge off. I didn't put it on in the first place to back away under fire from you or anybody else, Lee. So I'm not taking it off and I'm not through. In fact, I'm just starting."

Mosby's head came up and he pounded a heavy fist

on the desk top. "I say you're through! I hired you. Now I'm firing you!"

Their eyes met and held. In the same quiet tone, Allard murmured, "Think so, Lee? Well I don't."

Mosby's glance shifted, swung away. "Of all the damn fools!" he blurted. "You think you can make good on what you promised Lafe Oglevie? You think you can run Harry Shelline out of town? Didn't you hear what I was talking to Pinto Jardene about?"

"I heard. So—what?"

"How far did I get, suggesting that Shelline get out of sight for a time? Nowhere. Pinto said nothing doing."

"Well," drawled Allard, "in that case we'll just have to change Mister Jardene's mind for him."

"That's fool talk!" Mosby almost yelled the words. "We'll change nothing. Pinto Jardene runs this town. How many times do I have to tell you that? I know what his orders will be about you now. You're done! Give me that badge and be on your way. That'll make it easiest all around."

Allard sucked on his cigarette and let blue smoke dribble from his lips. "As I recall it, Jardene wanted the C Cross crew headed off. They were. So why should he get sore?"

"I'm not talking about that and you know it," Mosby snarled thickly. "You promised Oglevie something you can't make good on. If you try to make good, Pinto will cut you right off at the pockets. You didn't help matters a bit. You've only made them worse."

A frosty harshness came out of Allard again. "You miss the point entirely, Lee. I headed off Oglevie, not because Pinto Jardene wanted it that way, but because Oglevie and his crew were headed to step clear past the law of this town. You and me, it seems, have different ideas about what law is. To me, it's something that stands by itself, its code plain and easy to read. It's not something made up on the spur-of-the-moment by the orders of Pinto Jardene or anybody else."

Allard straightened in his chair and leaned forward. "Now get this. Like I said just now, I didn't put this badge on in the first place, just to take it off the minute some blown-up deadfall owner snaps his fingers. I don't answer to that sort of stuff like you do. As for Jardene cutting me off at the pockets, that could run into quite a chore." A hard rasp came into Allard's tone. "Goddamn it, Lee—why don't you get up off your belly and walk like a man, instead of crawling around in front of Pinto Jardene like a whipped dog?"

Lee Mosby's face fairly puffed out with congested crimson, and a wild anger hung explosively on his lips. But the chill and boring impact of Allard's eyes made him pause. Then, as was his usual way, Mosby sought refuge in temporizing.

"You don't know Pinto Jardene. You don't know how much weight he swings. You don't know what he can do."

"Maybe I don't know Jardene too well as an individual," retorted Allard. "But I do know the breed. And it's mongrel, Mosby. Nine times out of ten, when the chips are really down, it comes up mongrel. Jardene may be an exception. There's one way to find out. Stand up to him. Let him know who's really running this town. The law! And make it stick!"

"You just don't understand," mumbled Mosby. "Pinto's got backing—plenty! And there are others who see things just as he does. In this game you got to play along..."

Allard cut him off with a hard wave of his hand. "There's one thing, Mosby, that no man can do and come out whole. He can't play both ends against the middle. He can't be all things to all men. He's got to be one thing or the other."

The stubborn surliness in Mosby did not lessen. "There's a lot for you to learn, Allard," he blurted. "How long you been packing that badge? Less than twenty-four hours. Well, I been packing mine for going on two years. And I'm still doing all right."

The growing contempt in Allard's eyes deepened. In a way it was almost laughable, yet in a way it was pitiful. This burly hulk of a man trying to justify himself and his actions. Allard stood up and really used the whip.

"I suppose you figure you did all right out there against Lafe Oglevie and his C Cross crowd? Well, if you do, you got queer damn ideas about such things. For you crawled, Mosby, and you know it! Now, if you want to keep on crawling, that's all right with me. But don't try and tell me to hand over this badge and quit. That don't go. You're not taking it off me and neither is such as Pinto Jardene." He moved to the door and paused there. "I'm going over to give Mister Harry Shelline the bad news. Want to come along?"

Lee Mosby, smarting and fuming and surly under the lash, started to shake his head, hesitated, then lunged to his feet.

"Why not, Allard? I think I will. Just as a spectator, you understand. It's your brag. You made it. Now I want to see you put it across."

With the shank of the morning well along and the sun towering, the world was fair. Beyond town, the upsweep of the country leading to the Bench shimmered with clean, inviting distance. South, the long run of the plain lay empty, but green with the vigor of spring. Down there, so the word was, more trail herds were on the move, though as yet none were in sight.

Of all of this, the town of Pawnee was the hub, and at this moment apparently showed a clean face. But it was a false cleanliness. For behind it, hidden beyond doors of dives and deadfalls, lay a shoddy foulness. A dark and rapacious kingdom of which one Pinto Jardene was the accepted head.

Frank Allard mused on these things as he strode along. He was no reformer, no savior of souls. He knew men and their ways. He knew their strengths and their frailties, even as he knew his own. No man or woman was perfect. Virtue and vice were relative things, in all too many cases the products of circumstance or some quirk of fortune. Tears could be a common property, as could pain. So too could be discouragement and the disillusionment of blasted ideals and high hopes and dreams that had been shattered somewhere along the trail of life.

On his own part, the purpose behind his first seeking of this night marshal job had hardly been a lofty one. Baldly put, it was to aid in his seeking a personal vengeance. But he had given his word to Gil Paxton and Con Waters—also to Lafe Oglevie. Beyond all that, when he had first pinned on this badge, something else had come to him, a strange voltage that had traveled up his spine and squared his shoulders. He had committed himself to a cause, and now there was a cool pride burning in him that would not let him back away.

With Lee Mosby at his heels he stepped into the Palace. The place still echoed with comparative emptiness. The lone barman was fussing up and down with odd chores. Pinto Jardene stood leaning against the bar, eyes heavy and inscrutable, a half-smoked cheroot balanced in his fingers. Harry Shelline sat at a nearby table, dealing make-up hands, the cards slithering and flashing under the deft, trained touch of his mechanical practice.

Pinto Jardene put his glance on Allard for a moment, then moved it past him to Lee Mosby, following this with blunt words. "From what I could see of it from here, Mosby, you didn't look too good out there. But they turned back. Why?"

Mosby, coloring under the raw sarcasm in Jardene's words, jerked his head toward Frank Allard. "Ask him. His deal and his party all the way."

Jardene's eyes came back to Allard. "Well?"

Allard paid him no attention, moving over to the

table where the gambler sat. "Get your gear together, Shelline," he ordered curtly. "You're leaving town."

The flutter of cards stilled. Shelline's head tilted and he stared at Allard blankly. "Don't know what you mean." His voice was a thin drone.

Allard's tone sharpened. "I'll make it plainer. You're being given a floater, Shelline. You're not good for this town. So you're leaving Pawnee—for good. You got until sundown tonight to be gone. Can you understand that, or do I have to write it down for you?"

Pinto Jardene came swiftly away from the bar, his words an explosive exclamation. "Just a minute there—just a minute! What kind of damn fool talk is that? Who says Shelline is leaving town? Mosby, what are you trying—?"

"Not me," cut in Mosby heavily, shaking his head. "I'm just looking and listening. It's Allard's idea. His deal—all the way."

Anger was a gusty violence breaking from Pinto Jardene. "Then I've had a big plenty of this fellow Allard. Take that badge off him, Mosby, and kick him out!"

Allard came around then, his eyes hard and frosty. "Well, now," he drawled. "I'm just waiting for all that to happen."

"Mosby!" raged Jardene, "You heard what I said. Take that badge off him!"

"Why pick on Mosby?" taunted Allard. "You're the one who seems full of ambition. You try to take it off."

Ordinarily, Pinto Jardene gave orders, watched others do his bidding. It was part of the man's pose of power, never to mix in any sort of physical encounter. The king concept. Rough stuff was only for the hirelings to perform. But there was something about this Frank Allard, this rangy, cold-eyed man now defying him that enraged Pinto Jardene past all caution or usual conduct. He came in, cat fast, his left hand reaching out in a clawing sweep at the badge on Allard's shirt front, his right hand sliding under his coat toward his left armpit.

Neither hand reached its objective. That clawing left was knocked aside by a hard and heavy forearm. Then Allard's right shoulder hunched slightly and his fist smashed home to Jardene's face. The dive owner crashed back against the bar, bounced off, and went down in a rolling sprawl. Moving in swiftly, Allard pounced, grabbed the gun from the shoulder holster under Jardene's arm, then came up and around, the gun poised.

Harry Shelline, half-risen behind the poker table, dropped back into his chair. Lee Mosby, staring at the sprawled figure of Pinto Jardene in stark disbelief, neither moved or said a word. The bartender froze, after spreading both hands, palms down, on top of the bar before him.

Pinto Jardene had to make two tries of it before he could gain his feet. Even then he had to hang onto the bar for support. His mashed lips had already leaped out into a grotesque pout. His face was ash-gray except for twin spots of crimson burning in his smooth cheeks and for a smear of blood now beginning to seep from a corner of his mouth. His eyes were a dead-black.

Through them he stared at Frank Allard with a sort of blind fixity as though forever and forever he was placing that man deep in some dark pit of hatred. Then, without a word he turned and headed for the back room, sliding his hand along the edge of the bar to steady himself. He went through the door, closed it behind him.

Allard looked at the gambler, who sat motionless. "So maybe now you get the idea, Shelline. You'll be gone from town by tonight. Understand?"

When Shelline did not answer, Allard rolled up slightly on his toes, leaning forward. "Understand?"

Shelline nodded. "I understand."

Frank Allard turned and paused beside the still dazed and unbelieving Mosby, his voice curt.

"Well, you saw it done. Was it so damned hard, after all?"

Without waiting for an answer he went on out.

The bartender and Harry Shelline traded glances, then both looked at Mosby. Shelline spoke thinly.

"After that, you might as well turn in your badge, Mosby. Because Pinto's not going to like you at all. What kind of a game are you trying to play, anyhow?"

Lee Mosby shook his head, shook his shoulders, the act of a man trying to accept as real something he still had to believe was stark unreality. What couldn't be, had been, and it had taken place right before his eyes. And seeing it slowly stirred into being something that he had long believed dead—a single ember of pride, which had been lying dormant and almost forgotten under the tarnish of disuse. He looked at Shelline fixedly, and a strange half-smile pulled at his lips.

"No game at all, up to now, Shelline. But I just saw the first hand dealt in a new kind of game. And it interests me, it really does. And from what Frank Allard just told you, it looks like you won't be around to see the game played out."

Then Lee Mosby turned and left.

Harry Shelline got to his feet, looked at the door of the back room with some doubt. Then he shrugged. "Give me a bucket of water and a couple of bar towels, Chet."

The bartender handed over the desired articles. "You're welcome," he murmured. "Things will be savage in there."

Pinto Jardene was prowling the back room like something caged. He'd been dabbing at his swollen, bleeding mouth with a handkerchief. Now, when Shelline put the bucket of water and several towels on the table, Jardene moved up, wet a towel, and held it against his face. Shelline stood aside, keeping his silence. Presently, past the muffling towel, Pinto spoke.

"I want him dead, right on the floor in front of me. Then I'll stamp his face in while he lies there!"

Still the gambler held his silence and presently Pinto Jardene spoke again. "I lost my head in there and made a fool mistake. I'm not about to make another. We've had something slipped over on us, Harry. I had a queer hunch last night when they brought that fellow Allard in to introduce him as night marshal that something wasn't what it appeared to be. I didn't follow the hunch and say—no! Well, before I'm done with all of them they'll wish they hadn't been quite so damned smooth and smart."

Shelline cleared his throat. "You mean Gil Paxton and Con Waters?"

Jardene nodded. "Among others. There's Mosby, too."

In his thin and toneless way, the gambler said, "Understand me, Pinto; I never did cotton to Mosby, and I don't now. But I'll say this for him. I never saw a man more surprised and bewildered than Mosby was out front. I don't believe he was in on any kind of scheme—not to start with. But what happened out there has given him ideas. He's going to be harder to handle from here on out."

"He'll be handled," Jardene snapped bitterly. "You know where Plume Creek is?"

"Heard of it," admitted Shelline. "West somewhere, under the Bench rim."

"That's right. You keep following under the curve of the Bench to the west and you can't miss it. That's where you're going. You'll find Ned Fargo and his boys camped there. You stay with them until you hear from me."

"I don't like the idea of pulling a runout," Shelline objected. "A thing like that can follow a man forever."

Jardene looked at Shelline over a wadded towel. "He

gave you a floater, didn't he? You think you could stick and play the hand by yourself?"

Shelline shrugged. "Allard's mortal. I can fix it so he'll have to come to me, and I can be set for him, too."

Jardene gave the gambler another look past the wadded towel. "You got your own brand of guts, Harry. But just now you're not using your head anymore than I used mine a few minutes ago. You're still thinking in terms of that hunk of saffron, Lee Mosby. But this fellow Allard is a different breed entirely. We'd be fools not to realize that he's smart and tough and dangerous, and that we've got to play him as such. We got plenty of time. We'll make damn sure of our next move. We'll let him believe that he's got us buffaloed, let him pile up some false confidence. Then, when we're ready, we'll cut him down to size in a hurry. So, you're heading for Plume Creek."

The dive owner soaked another towel, held the compress to his lips. The bitter blackness of his eyes did not change as he mumbled. "Yeah, I want him on the floor in front of me—dead as hell!"

CHAPTER FIVE

GIL PAXTON cradled his coffee cup in both hands and looked past it at Frank Allard. "If I was good at words I'd give a toast to the first piece of real law enforcement this town has seen in a long, long time."

Allard shrugged. "I did it mainly to head off a ruckus with Lafe Oglevie and the C Cross outfit. It was the only thing I could think of at the time to keep the pot from boiling over."

The storekeeper drank deep, put his cup down, and wiped his lips with the back of his hand. "Just the same, it was a big satisfaction to see Harry Shelline riding out of town with all his gear. That's due to make a lot of others stop and think."

They were sitting at the supper table in Gil Paxton's living quarters, in the second story of his store building.

The girl, Nell, had served them. Now, after clearing away most of the dishes, she was busy with these in the adjacent kitchen. As Allard turned his head slightly toward the sound of her industry, Paxton spoke dryly.

"Been a heap of help to me, Nell has. Her father was Luke Kane, who set up as a small-time rancher on the Bench. But he had the bad habit of getting a little bit too free and easy with the cattle of other men. So he was eventually found hanging to a tree limb. Nell was fourteen at the time. She didn't know which way to turn, so I took her in to keep house for me and to give her a decent home. That was six years ago."

The girl came in, poured Allard a final cup of coffee. At that moment a bell tinkled down in the store. Paxton pushed back from the table, exclaiming with slight irritation. "Always, just at eating time, there has to be a customer of some sort. Don't hurry, Frank. Finish your coffee."

The girl, about to return to the kitchen, paused and listened to the sound of Paxton's descending steps on the stairs down to the store. Then she turned back, put the coffee pot on the table, and stood looking at Allard. For the first time she spoke directly to him.

"So right now you're the big man of this town."

The words were startling, and for a moment Allard stared at her. The lamplight was such that her eyes were shadowed, and he could read nothing of her thoughts. She was well and fully developed, this girl, vital as a sullen young animal. Allard answered her with a careful brevity.

"Not too big. Not big at all."

"Yes, you are," she insisted. "And it must be a fine feeling to be somebody. To really be somebody. And to be free—free! And not in prison..."

Allard waited, watching her carefully.

"You see," she went on, "I'm in a prison. In two of them. Daughter of a cow thief, that's me. John Chan-

64

cellor hung my father for stealing cattle. That puts me in one kind of prison. The other one is right here where I'm standing. Oh, according to his lights, Mister Paxton has been kind enough to me, I guess. He's fed me and given me a home of sorts. He's treated me decent. But he can't seem to understand that those things aren't everything. For himself it's enough just to run his store, have three meals a day, and a comfortable place to sleep at night. But there must be more to life than just that." She paused before adding a little fiercely, "One of these days I'm going to break out of this prison!"

Frank Allard tried to keep all of this in proper perspective. This girl, who had been silent and somewhat sullen all through the forepart of the evening, was now, in a sudden rush of dammed-up feeling, giving him, a virtual stranger, certain confidences. It was a brand new, startling experience. It could even be leading up to a plea of some sort. So now, as he answered her, he spoke with a soothing wariness.

"Life can be pretty monotonous at times for all of us, Nell."

She had moved around the table, closer to him. Now she leaned abruptly, framed his face in her hands, kissed him full on the mouth. The hot and fiery shock of it ran clear down to his heels. He twisted out of his chair, came to his feet. The girl stepped back and stood with folded arms, watching him.

"You'll probably never understand why I did that," she said calmly. "Maybe I'm not quite sure myself. Oh, I know exactly what you're thinking and you're completely wrong. I'm not that sort at all. At least not yet. And I hope," she added, with a twisted, bitter little smile, "that I never will be. But it could be one way of breaking out of prison. Yes, you're somebody in this town now. By kissing you, maybe that makes me somebody, too."

To steady himself, Allard concentrated on twisting

up a cigarette while speaking with some harshness. "You're a silly little baggage!"

She showed that twisted smile again. "Am I? Well, maybe I am. But I'm also smart enough to see kindness in a man. It's in you. There was another man who was kind. His name was Jim Creightly. He understood how a person could be lonely, so lonely that at times they wouldn't care what happened to them, just so they weren't lonely anymore. And this town k-killed Jim Creightly!"

Her voice broke slightly. She caught up the coffee pot and ran into the kitchen.

Frank Allard's face was grave and expressionless as he went down to the store. Standing in front of the counter, Gil Paxton was talking to Haley and Royce Twitchell. There was some kind of acid feeling stirred between the three of them, and Paxton's voice was curt as he turned to the sound of Allard's step.

"Here he is now, Twitchell. Suppose you say it to his face."

The Twitchells, father and son, came around to face Allard. It was young Royce who spoke with his usual sarcasm. "The man of the moment—the bucko boy! Shall I tell him, or will you, Dad?"

Allard looked Royce Twitchell up and down coldly. "I suggest that you don't try and tell me anything, friend. For there's nothing about you that I like. Your tone, your looks—nothing! Hell with you!" His glance moved on to the stocky, red-faced banker, the elder Twitchell. "Well?"

Haley Twitchell had the usual badly chewed rag of a cigar in his mouth, with the usual brown stain rimming his lips. He showed some restlessness under the impact of Allard's chilly gaze, and he moved over to the store stove and disposed of his soggy cigar butt before answering.

"It's like this, Allard," he said carefully. "We've got a pretty nice little town here, all things considered.

Everything running smooth and comfortable. Oh, we've a few rough edges, but that's true of any trail-town. Now about that—er—affair in the Palace today..."

"All right—what about it?" cut in Allard. "Why should any part of it hurt your feelings?"

Haley Twitchell's red face took on even a deeper shade. A heavy note crept into his voice. "Shall we say it was an unfortunate occurrence—and unnecessary? Your authority, Allard, hardly extends that far. I should have thought Lee Mosby would have made that clear to you."

There wasn't a single shred of mirth in Allard's harsh laugh. "My authority, Twitchell, extends just as far as I figure necessary. Now don't try to tell me that this town of Pawnee is going to miss the presence of a cheap tinhorn like Shelline."

"We weren't thinking about Harry Shelline," blurted Royce Twitchell. "It's one thing to run a small-time gambler out of town. It's something else to rough up a man like Pinto Jardene. Just how big do you think that badge has made you, Allard?"

"Plenty big enough to keep on wearing it," was Allard's cold retort. "Jardene tried to yank the badge off me and at the same time was set to pull a gun. I could have killed him with full lawful reason. He got off easy, all things considered. Now would you like to try your hand at the same deal?"

Whatever it was the Twitchells saw in Frank Allard's eyes, it was enough to keep them silent. Allard let a considerable interval of time run, then moved on to the door. Over his shoulder he said, "Obliged for the meal, Gil. Enjoyed it."

Another silence held the store until the sound of Allard's departing steps faded out. Then, with a small smile, Gil Paxton murmured, "Now you know, gentlemen."

The glint that shone in Haley Twitchell's eyes was baleful. He spoke heavily. "You and Con Waters put something over on us, Paxton. We'll remember that fact. Come on, Royce."

The banker turned and stamped out. Young Twitchell lingered for a moment, fuming. "That fellow Allard won't be around long. Not long!"

"Why bother to say that to me?" retorted Paxton calmly. "Yapping behind a man's back means nothing. You just had a chance to say everything to his face. You didn't. So big words now are empty as hell."

Cursing, Royce Twitchell went along after his father.

Gil Paxton stood for a little time, a troubled frown on his face. Finally he shrugged and sighed. He decided to close up early and go have a talk with Con Waters.

Taking his ease on his bunk in the stable's harness room, Con listened quietly to what Gil Paxton had to tell him. Then he chuckled softly. "I'd have enjoyed seeing Allard make the Twitchells take water. Their self-imagined size irritates me at times. And we must back Allard as we promised, Gil."

"Of course," agreed Paxton. "But what puzzles me is why the Twitchells should be walking stiff-legged just because Pinto Jardene ran into Allard's fist. Although the three of them are together a great deal, I've never felt that there was any great love between them. More of a fellowship of convenience, or something of the sort, I'd call it. So I sometimes wonder if there are not more things afoot than meets the eye."

"Now," agreed Con thoughtfully, "you may have something there. This we know. Haley Twitchell has the money and money can reach into many dark places. Could be that Twitchell owns a major part of the Palace, and he figures that Allard's move was therefore as much against him as it was against Pinto Jardene? Yes, there are many possibilities at which we can only guess. But this I am sure of. In Jardene and the Twitchells you see three men who could never have any real trust of mine, as I see in all of them a broad streak of rascal."

"Just so," Gil Paxton said. "And Haley Twitchell left the store with something of a threat hanging in the air. He said that you and I had put something over on them and that they'd be remembering it."

Con Waters pulled to his feet and took a couple of turns up and down the little room. "Well," he said, "we did put something over on them, didn't we? Also, as a lawyer might say it—with malice aforethought. But I don't know what they can do about it, Gil. Neither of us owe Twitchell money, and we owe Jardene less. So I refuse to worry. I'm too old to worry about a threat."

Frank Allard had hoped to find the office empty, as he wanted to sit alone and in the dark, with just his smoke and his thoughts. For there were still some vastly disturbing ones. That girl—that Nell Kane! How was a man to figure her? Despite the brazen boldness of her action there had still been a certain honesty in her words both before and after her startling act. So reserved opinion seemed to be the fairest conclusion.

Lee Mosby's voice hit at him from the dark depths of the office. "You're damned careless, Allard, after what happened today. I could have been Harry Shelline, waiting for you with a sawed-off shotgun. Just because Shelline rode out of town is no reason he couldn't have cut back as soon as it got dark."

Allard, startled, was still for a moment. "You could be right," he admitted. He felt his way to a chair and sat down. Silence held for a little time before Mosby spoke again.

"Where do you and I stand, Allard?"

"That," Allard told him, "is something you'll have to figure your own answer to."

He heard Mosby's heavy, troubled sigh. "Already have, just about. You intend to hang onto that badge?"

"That's right."

By this time Allard had Mosby well-located, and he

sensed no danger in the man. He relaxed in his chair. "I wouldn't worry about it too much," he drawled. "After all, both Jardene and Twitchell passed on me. You can always hold them to that fact."

"Maybe yes, maybe no," said Mosby slowly. "You're supposed to be working under me, taking my orders. Yet you do as you damn well please. Where does that leave me?"

"Giving the wrong orders, maybe." Allard turned a little curt. "It'd be quite simple if you ran your office straight up and down and to hell with what Pinto Jardene or Haley Twitchell think. They're not the whole voice in this town."

"Maybe not," agreed Mosby. "But they're still a big chunk of it. Still and all..." His words ran out and his chair creaked as he stirred restlessly. "Damn you, Frank Allard—you're like a long forgotten conscience, surging up all of a sudden and spurring hell out of a man. Took today to make me realize how far I'd slipped from what I'd once been. Sure makes me feel anything but proud. Yet I find I still got a little live blood in me. I found that out when I watched you cut Jardene and Shelline down to size. They proved not half as big as they once seemed to be. So—maybe..." Mosby's voice trailed off again.

Allard leaned forward in his chair. "So—what?"

"Why," said Mosby, "it could be that I'll surprise the natives. Yes, sir—I barely might do just that. We'll see, the next time Pinto Jardene or either of the Twitchells try to look down their noses at me and order me around. Somebody might be told to go to hell, and like it!"

Allard laughed with soft exultancy. "Man, I apologize. I've been thinking wrong things about you."

Mosby grunted. "Now don't go changing your opinion too fast. Maybe I don't weigh as much as I'm beginning to think I do. But it'll be interesting to find out. What say we make the rounds together? Looks like another quiet night ahead, so we won't lose out on too much sleep."

They made the rounds. They looked in at dives and deadfalls, and everywhere they met a sultry, sullen quiet. The word of the day's happenings had spread, and Frank Allard drew many a hard and measuring glance, but all such tempered with caution.

On his part Allard was mainly interested in observing Lee Mosby's new attitude. Here was change that was surprising, but satisfying. There was more upright certainty in the marshal's stride, less of the lunging shamble. Mosby carried his head higher, his shoulders straighter. His glance was level, steadier. Whether the change was false or real, only Mosby in his heart knew. Allard would have to wait for more certain proof.

In the Palace things were almost ominously orderly. There was no sign of Pinto Jardene, and the other habitués of the place showed a cautious disinterest in Allard and Mosby as they moved up to the bar and had a short drink together. The bartender served them as he might have a pair of strangers. When they went out into the night's chilling darkness again, Mosby made a sarcastic comment.

"Must be an awful change in my appearance. That barkeeper has poured plenty of drinks for me in the past. Tonight you'd have thought he'd never seen me before."

"About this time last night you were telling me that a lawman's life was a dog's life," reminded Allard. "The sort of deal where you're damned if you do and damned if you don't. I guess it all depends on what you'd rather be damned for, Lee."

Back up in his room, Allard was finishing a cigar before turning in for the night, when a knock sounded at the door. It was Ben Ripon, and he carried a glass of steaming toddy.

"Nightcap," said the little hotel owner. "My compliments."

Allard, startled, said, "Now that's damned kind of you, Ben. But why?"

The little man looked him straight in the eye. "You slapped Pinto Jardene down, didn't you? And ran Harry Shelline out of town? Well, I liked both those things."

Ben Ripon paused in the doorway. "I've been around these parts for a considerable time. Should you ever have any questions needing answers, mebbe I might help. G'night!"

Allard sipped his toddy slowly, savoring each mouthful, his thoughts touching on all the varied events of the day, and it came to him that where people were concerned, a man never knew where he might strike good metal or poor, turn up an enemy or a friend. With Ben Ripon it had been a friend.

Again, a sense of support, after a man had walked long alone, could awaken a moral fiber grown almost atrophied, as in Lee Mosby's case. A flame, it seemed, once fanned alight, could catch on and burn in the most unexpected of places.

Allard did not get to sleep as easily as the previous night. He thought of Nell Kane and of the sudden caress she had given him, and of the meaning of the words she had used to justify that act. Somehow she'd seemed completely honest about it. But it had been a disturbing situation.

He thought of what she had said about Jim Creightly. A kind man she had called him, and one who could understand the meaning of loneliness. How far, Allard wondered, did that meaning reach? Had there been anything between her and Creightly?

Even though a complete realist where human nature was concerned, Frank Allard knew a swift repugnance at this thought. For, though Nell Kane was actually a young woman physically, in many ways she seemed little more than a somewhat bitter and rebellious child. Still, you never knew....

Allard shook his head angrily. After all, Jim Creightly

was dead, and all the memories Allard had of him were good ones. Better to keep them so. Of one thing Allard was certain. Speaking of Creightly as she had, proved that the girl had known Creightly rather well. Therefore something she might be able to tell him could well throw possible light on the cause behind Creightly's death. When the right chance offered, Allard decided, he'd ask her some questions on this.

With the warmth of the toddy taking hold, Allard began to doze. And now, queerly enough, the picture of another girl came into his mind...Barbara Chancellor. Here was no sultriness, no problems of mixed-up repressions and jangled emotions.

Beyond a doubt Barbara Chancellor had problems of her own. Like the responsibility of running a big ranch, or of hauling a dead man home in the back of her wagon, or trying to head off a crew bent on extracting violent vengeance over that dead man. But these were exterior things. Inwardly she knew no emotional warps or twists. This girl had the straightforward impact on a man of a vigorous breeze sweeping down from the high Bench country where she rode and lived.

When Frank Allard went down to breakfast the next morning, he was startled to see Lafe Oglevie at a table talking to Ben Ripon. The C Cross foreman showed his lion's grin and tipped a beckoning hand. Ben Ripon stood up and shoved his chair out invitingly to Allard.

"Been telling Lafe about things," said Ripon. "Sit here, Mister Allard. I like to see two good men eating together."

Allard took the chair, and the little hotel owner went on about his business. Lafe Oglevie rumbled, "Well, you kept your word."

"Generally try to," returned Allard laconically. "Plain truth of it is—you left me with damn little choice."

Lafe Oglevie worked on his coffee cup, then put it aside with a sigh. "Let me tell you this, friend. I was sure relieved to have a reasonable proposition offered me. Bluntly, I was way out on a limb and plenty shaky. Because the last thing in the world that I wanted was to see a general ruckus start, and the boys would sure have forced my hand. But you opened an alley for me to slide out through."

"You had Miss Chancellor pretty badly worried," reminded Allard.

Oglevie nodded. "Yeah, I know. Sorry about it, too. But the crew was all ready to bust things wide open, to really rip and tear. Most generally I can keep them pretty well in line, but I could see that this was one time when I couldn't. So where do you stand if the crew you're bossing looks you in the eye and tells you they're going to do a thing, whether you like it or not? What answer do you give them—and what do you do?"

"What you did, I guess," Allard conceded. "You ride along and do what you can to keep things under control. Either that, or you fire them."

"You don't fire them, not when they're a good crew," Oglevie said. "You just try and figure a sensible answer of some sort and hope for a break that will clear matters up before things get too rough. You offered that break."

"You were a little rough on Lee Mosby," Allard pointed out.

Lafe Oglevie grunted. "He's had a spurring coming for quite some time. No backbone there, not none at all."

"Don't be too sure," Allard murmured. "A man can grow up."

A waitress brought Allard's breakfast and he went at it hungrily. "That fellow—Lark, you called him—hope his feelings aren't hurt too badly. I didn't enjoy mauling him around, but he would have it that way."

"He'll get over it," Oglevie assured comfortably.

"Good boy, Lark is—just a mite on the fiery side. Flick Lester was that type, too, which was what probably got him killed. Understand, nobody hated to lose Flick more than I did. But a man can't pile as many summers on his head as I got on mine without being practical about such things. Knowing Flick as I did, I wouldn't no way be surprised if the real facts would show that he did force that gun deal with Shelline. Also, that he probably went for his gun first. And when a man does that, why then he's got to finish the ride, regardless."

Lafe Oglevie built a smoke before going on in a slow, thoughtful way. "Not that I'm making a case for Shelline, understand. For he's all crooked and a damn tinhorn, much too slick with both cards and a gun. The day somebody beats him to the first shot, that day the world will be better off. But Flick Lester knew Shelline for what he was, yet sat into a game with him. He might have known he'd get trimmed."

"In short," Allard asked, "If a man loses out because of something that figures up as being mainly his own fault, you don't figure his friends as being justified in going all out for vengeance, is that it?"

"Close enough." Lafe Oglevie's glance was level and sober. "I saw a man hung once for a crime he was innocent of. He might have deserved being hung for something else he'd done some other time, but the charge that strung him wasn't the one. And I just don't go for that sort of thing. Oh, I know it's a rough world, and I've been pretty rough a time or two myself. Mebbe I will again, before I die. But there is a right and there is a wrong, and me, I try to keep both where they belong."

Allard nodded. "Pretty much my own sentiments." With a small grin, he added, "Always making allowances of course, for a certain amount of ornery human nature."

Lafe Oglevie chuckled. "Just so."

Frank Allard, liking what he'd seen in this man from the first, found that regard deepening. There was a rugged, fundamental honesty in Lafe Oglevie, a sense of balance and a breadth of understanding of men and their ways that only the experience of the years plus an innate soundness of character could give.

"Aiming to stay in town long?" Allard asked.

"Pulling out right away," Oglevie said. "I've found out what I came to town for. As you promised, Shelline is on his way. The fact that you put a fist into Pinto Jardene's face is an added satisfaction. When I tell these things to the boys, I'll have a quiet crew again." Oglevie's glance keened. "About Pinto Jardene, you've started something there. He'll hate you forever and clear past hell. I always understood that he was the big boss in this town. So can't understand why he didn't have you fired."

"Maybe," said Allard quietly, "I don't fire easy."

Oglevie, grave for a moment, grinned faintly. "Good man! Should things shape up any time when you need a mite of help, let me know."

"Fair enough, and obliged," Allard said. "I'll do that." Then he added, "I was figuring on a little ride this morning to sort of get the lay of the country. Mind if I hit the out trail with you for a ways?"

Oglevie answered heartily, "Nothing I'd like better."

It was good to have a horse between his knees again. The roan, rested and full fed, was eager to be on the move again and had an easy swing to its stride. From well up on the slope north of town, Allard twisted in his saddle and looked back.

Pawnee was a sprawling blot on a country that spread lush with spring's fresh greenness as far as the eye could reach. The railroad was a faint line of sun glitter, and along this, rolling in from the east, was a toy train of cattle cars.

North, the world had a lift of free vastness. This was the Bench, a long running plateau, bulwarked finally by a humpbacked range of timber-darkened mountains. Lafe Oglevie marked the glint of appreciation in Frank Allard's searching gaze.

"Good country. None better. But like all good country, marked with the curse of a few of the breed that never seem to learn to leave well enough alone. So, at times, we have our troubles."

Allard flashed Oglevie a quick glance, wondering about this. Oglevie went on, speaking with the slow soberness of a man picking his words and thoughts carefully.

"When a man gets to know a country as well as I know this one, and when he gets to know the pulse of its everyday run of affairs, then he can sort of sense a change in the atmosphere, you might say. He doesn't have to hear anything or see anything special—he just sort of feels it. Well, there's something shaping up in these parts that I feel and don't like. Don't ask me exactly what it is, because I don't know. But it's there, just the same. Sound crazy to you?"

"Not at all," Allard answered. "Know what you mean. Like you can feel a change coming up in the weather, even though the sun is shining and the sky clear."

Lafe Oglevie bobbed his head. "That's it exactly. For instance, I understand that Ned Fargo has a camp over on Plume Creek and that he's got some half-dozen hard case riders with him. Well then, some sound cattlemen ran Ned Fargo off the Hospice Grant range a full year ago. Now he turns up here, and a man wonders—why?"

Allard was silent for a moment, his thoughts reaching back to his first night in Pawnee when Gil Paxton introduced him to five men gathered around a poker table in the back room of the Palace. Paxton had named one of those men as Ned Fargo. A rider, and hardly one to admire or view with respect as Allard recalled.

"Why was this Fargo hombre given the run-out off that other range?"

"Cattle. The other fellow's," rumbled Oglevie. "Far as I know, since he hit Plume Creek, he's just sat quiet. Which ain't natural, for I doubt he's got money enough to retire on." The C Cross foreman fixed Allard with a direct glance. "You're wondering of course, why I'm telling you this. Well, I like to believe I'm a pretty fair judge of men, and from what I've seen of you I'd rate you as solid and sound. Carrying that badge, you're going to be around Pawnee a lot. You're bound to hear things and see things. And should you happen to run across anything that could tie in with what I've been telling of—such as to why Ned Fargo is hanging around—I'd take it kindly if you'd pass the word along to me. How about it?"

"Of course—and glad to," Allard replied. "Am I guessing, or are you suggesting that this fellow Fargo could have some connections in town?"

"Anything," was the rumbling answer, "can come out of a nest of crooks. And Pawnee has got more than its legitimate share of that breed."

Up ahead a rider lifted into view, coming on at a fast jog. It was Barbara Chancellor, making a fine and invigorating picture as she sat on her saddle with a sure and practiced ease, lending of her own natural grace to the horse beneath her. As she reined in to face them, her expression was one of mingled curiosity and relief. She scolded Lafe Oglevie mildly.

"Lafe, you worry me to death. I had to go to the boys to find out where you'd been off to so early this morning. You might have let me know."

Oglevie's lion grin held a fondness as he looked at her. "Well, it was like this. Me and Allard here, we made a little deal yesterday. I just wanted to see how it had worked out. I was intending to let you know as soon as I got back to the ranch. Girl, you quit worrying about me. I'm old enough to take care of myself."

"That was what Flick Lester thought." Her words and manner were sober. "And how did that deal you mentioned work out?"

"Just fine! I'd even say—wonderful! Harry Shelline left for other parts and Pinto Jardene is nursing a sore mug." The grizzled foreman's grin became a growling chuckle. "I understand that friend Allard here really laid one on Mister Jardene. I'd loved to have seen that."

The girl looked at Allard. "You actually laid hands on Pinto Jardene?"

Allard shifted a little in his saddle. "You might call it that."

"Might call it that," Lafe Oglevie mimicked, his shoulders shaking with inner mirth. "Man! From the way I heard it, you hit Jardene so hard he bounced!"

The interest in the girl's eyes deepened. "And you still wear your badge, Mister Allard?"

"Thought I'd hang onto it for a while yet," Allard told her briefly.

He met her glance so steadily she colored slightly and looked away, turning both her glance and her words to Lafe Oglevie again.

"You get along home, Lafe, and give the crew the word, so they'll settle down and start working again. The same goes for you. And if you ever go outside my orders again I'll fire the whole lot of you!"

Oglevie's eyes twinkled. "Now you're getting tough. Where you heading, youngster?"

"To town. I'm off to have another talk with that Kane girl and see if I can get her to consider selling me the old Kane range. If I'm not home by dark, don't fret. I may decide to stay in town overnight."

"There you go," grumbled Oglevie. "Here I'm a man grown and I can't hit town without you going into a stew of worry. Yet you figure it's quite all right for you to hang around that place. Now there's a couple more herds due up the trail at any time so I hear, and when they arrive, then Pawnee will be running over with crazy, wild trail hands. Think I'll ride back and keep an eye on you."

"You'll do nothing of the sort," defied the girl. "I'm going to town for strictly business reasons. While you're going home for the same reason—to get at the business of working cattle."

Lafe Oglevie grumbled some more. "From the time you were a little splinter of a kid I never could get anywhere trying to argue with you." He turned to Allard. "How about you filling in for me? Keep an eye on her, I mean?"

Barbara Chancellor flared immediately. "Nonsense! I don't need anyone to keep an eye on me." She lifted her reins and rode on.

Allard spoke softly. "Were you joshing, Lafe—or did you really mean I should take you at your word?"

"Little bit of both," growled Oglevie.

Allard spun his horse. "Just so, Lafe. And understood."

The roan's long-reaching lope brought Allard up beside Barbara Chancellor's jogging mount. As the girl glanced at him, Allard smiled faintly. "Orders," he explained. "Hope you don't mind?"

Her retort was tart. "It's a free road." A moment later she showed a warming smile. "I don't mean to be ungracious. But Lafe can be such a problem at times. My own fault, I suppose. I've spoiled him terribly."

"A good man," drawled Allard quietly. "A very good man."

"Yes," she agreed soberly, "he is. There are times when I wouldn't know what to do if I didn't have Lafe Oglevie to lean on."

"He's been with you a long time?"

She nodded. "A very long time. In fact, just about as far back as I can remember. He was Dad's right-hand man, and since Dad's death he's been invaluable to me."

Silence fell, except for the running mutter of steadily moving hoofs and the occasional creak of saddle gear. The sun poured down and the earth pushed its greenness up to meet it. A prairie finch winged by, its song a mite of free ecstasy. The world at the moment was a very fair and pleasant place indeed.

Barbara Chancellor was unconsciously reacting to the charm. She'd taken off her hat and hung it on her saddle horn. The sun glinted on her head and her face was soft and relaxed. Different indeed thought Allard, from the first time he'd seen her, on that gray, drenched, gloomy afternoon when she had driven away from Gil Paxton's store with a dead man in the back of her spring wagon.

On her part, Barbara Chancellor managed several guarded glances at the man riding beside her. He was rangy and tall and solid-looking. She wondered at the fixed taciturnity of his face in repose. It was an expression that hid so much of him.

"How," she asked suddenly, "did you happen to take on as night marshal?"

"A man needs a job," Allard answered carefully. "He comes across one. He takes it."

This, she was certain, was not all the answer, but in Allard's manner and words there was a certain warding off, which more or less closed a door on her, so she did not press the point. After all, though she admitted to a deepening interest in the man, he was still a virtual stranger, and common courtesy established a limit to her spoken curiosity.

They rode again in silence and in time the sprawled outlines of Pawnee took shape below them. And now there was something new down there, a slow moving blot of variegated color seeping up toward the cattle pens and loading yards south of town. Glimpsing this, Allard rocked a little higher in his saddle.

"Trail herd arriving," he said briefly.

Barbara Chancellor watched for a time, nodding. "I shouldn't resent them, I suppose, but I do. No doubt they bring prosperity to some, but they've changed things as I knew them for so long. I liked the country better as it was."

"Know what you mean," said Allard. "We work to set things up as we like them, and then something moves in to scramble the picture. All life is change and readjustment, I reckon."

She threw him a startled glance. Here was a bit of concise philosophy from an unexpected source. Perhaps that taciturn mask hid unguessed depths. They took the dropping angle of the sloped road and moved into town. At the road and street junction, Barbara Chancellor slowed her mount.

"I want to thank you again for the way you handled matters yesterday. It brings back some of the confidence I'd just about lost in this town and its ways. It is comforting to know that some vestige of law remains."

The faint shadow of a smile loosened the line of Allard's lips. "Thanks for letting me ride in with you. It's been very pleasant."

Again the directness of his glance sent the betraying flush of color through her cheeks and she urged her horse to a quickened pace. She knew a gust of impatience with herself. This man had the power to disturb her and she resented that.

Allard reined the roan the other way, toward Con Waters' stable.

Two people observed the arrival of Frank Allard and Barbara Chancellor. At the window of the bank, Royce Twitchell stood scowling, and as it followed Allard, his glance was murky. In the doorway of Gil Paxton's store, Nell Kane was a picture of indolent grace, and also of sullen, sultry discontent, which deepened as she watched. Riding past on his way to the stable, Allard looked at her, his head inclining slightly as he touched his hat.

Nell showed no sign of recognition, but her glance followed Barbara Chancellor as the latter rode up to Ben Ripon's hotel, swung down, and tied her horse. In Nell Kane's eyes burned a settled, bitter hatred.

CHAPTER SIX

ON THE LETTERHEADS of the Pawnee Mercantile Bank, Royce Twitchell's name was bolstered by the title of vice-president. It sounded important but actually meant very little, as most of the citizens of Pawnee were well aware. Haley Twitchell, the father, as president of the bank, was the bank—and he ran it as he ran his son, completely dominant. But it pleased the father to list the son's name in importance, even if it was an empty title.

In a small side office, off his father's larger one, Royce Twitchell paced restlessly up and down, finally stopping and facing the girl seated beyond the desk.

"This," he said, "is just one of those things you can't hurry, Barbara. On her own account, Nell Kane might have been willing to make a deal on that property long ago. But bringing Gil Paxton around to agreeing is something else again. And while I doubt he actually has the right to run that girl's affairs for her, it would take a lot of time and considerable money to prove it. All we can do is keep pressing the point with him and hope to finally wear down his resistance. You don't actually need that old Kane range right now, do you?"

"No-o," answered Barbara Chancellor slowly. "Perhaps I don't. But I can see the time coming when I will. And I don't want anyone else to get there ahead of me. I don't mean that as selfishly as it may sound. But I'm remembering something Dad always preached. He said that every real cattle ranch had natural limits, and that it wasn't complete until those natural limits were reached. Well, the old Kane range is the natural limit of the C Cross. If it's a question of price with Gil Paxton, I'm willing to go a little higher."

Royce Twitchell shook his head. "I don't feel that it is a question of price. It's just some idea Paxton has of holding the property against the Kane girl's future."

"I wonder," murmured Barbara. "Maybe the girl has more to say about it than you think. I tried to talk to her a little while ago and just couldn't get anywhere. Nell Kane hates me fiercely, and I don't know why."

Royce Twitchell looked out the window. "Maybe she can't forget how her father died."

Instantly Barbara flared. "Dad had nothing to do with the lynching of Luke Kane. Oh, I know the talk that went around, but Dad gave me his word that he wasn't there, or had a hand in it at all. And I'll believe that against all the loose talk in the world. You don't believe my father did it, do you?"

Royce Twitchell shrugged. "Somebody lynched Luke Kane. And it's left his daughter pretty bitter, which is understandable." He came around to face Barbara again, abruptly changing the point of discussion. "I didn't know you were so well acquainted with that hard-case drifter, Frank Allard."

Barbara's head came up, startled. "Well acquainted with him? I don't know what you mean."

"You rode into town with him a little while ago, didn't you?" There was a certain note of accusation here, and it struck another spark in the girl, bringing a quick, blunt retort.

"What's wrong with that? He's a comparative stranger, yes. But I've met him. And he was with Lafe Oglevie out along the trail, just about to turn back for town. So he rode back with me. It was as simple as that."

"Did he have to? Couldn't he have kept on riding with Oglevie?"

The spark grew, became a flash in Barbara's eyes. "Royce, I don't like your tone. After all, it's my affair alone who does or doesn't ride with me!"

Twitchell, recognizing definite danger signs, stopped his pacing to again stare out of the window. "Maybe it is, Barbara. But I do feel I'm entitled to question any acquaintance of yours with a fellow like Allard."

"For goodness sakes, why? Just what is there about Frank Allard that is so wrong?"

"Well, for one thing, nobody knows where he came from or what's along his back trail."

"All the more reason why he shouldn't be condemned without a hearing," charged Barbara. "The less you know of anyone, the more unfair it is to judge them, in particular to their disadvantage."

Royce came around. "You defending the man, Barbara?"

She tossed her head. "From what I've seen of Frank Allard, he seems quite capable of defending himself. Now this I know. So far, his contact with Pinto Jardene and that foul gambler, Shelline, has been such as to make them come to heel. Has anyone else done as much? No! For that matter, I understand that you play poker with them and that both you and your father are on quite friendly terms with them. So I think any unbiased observer would rate Frank Allard's attitude toward them as much the better one."

Royce Twitchell reddened and his lips showed an angry twist. However, he managed a deprecatory laugh. "In our position, my father and I have to get along with the powers that be. Men must do strange things in the name of business."

Barbara's glance became very direct as she studied him. In the past a certain friendship had grown up between her and Royce Twitchell. He wasn't a bad-looking sort at all and, up to now, his attitude toward her had been pleasantly gallant. But here, whether he was showing more of his real self than ever before, or whether she was seeing with a new keenness, Barbara felt that she was glimpsing something she didn't like. She got to her feet and moved to the door.

"I just can't imagine any business that could justify being on pleasant terms with Pinto Jardene and Harry Shelline or any other men like them, Royce."

Before he could answer she had slipped through the door and was gone. For several long moments Royce Twitchell stared at the empty doorway, after which he let his banked-up feelings go in a burst of low-toned cursing. He was still giving way to this when his father came in. Haley Twitchell stared at his son accusingly.

"What the devil went on in here? When Barbara Chancellor left this bank just now she was packing a considerable huff."

Royce shrugged sullenly. "Things we couldn't agree on."

"Personalities, I suppose?" charged the elder Twitchell. "That girl came in here to talk business and business alone. Why didn't you stick to business?"

Royce shrugged again, saying nothing.

"I think," rapped his father harshly, "that I've coddled you too damn much and for too damn long. One of these days I'm liable to chuck you out on the street, completely on your own. Then we'll see whether it will be sink or swim. "Can't you get it through your thick head that this is no four-bit poker hand we're playing? This hand is for big stakes—damn big stakes. I suggest you hunt up that girl and spread the honey on just as thick as you can!"

Saying which, Haley Twitchell stamped out, slamming the door.

At the cattle yards, all was noise and a certain ordered confusion. The bellowing of cattle was one long plaint, cut through now and then by the shrill yipping of some saddle hand who was swinging a lariat end or using a prod pole to harry critters up the loading chute and into the slatted cattle car beyond. A locomotive hissed and snorted as it switched empty cars into place and pulled loaded ones away. Car couplings rattled and thumped and squealed rustily, and the bell of the locomotive beat out a monotonous brassy clanging. The air smelled of coal smoke and of hot bovine odors.

Standing off to one side, Lee Mosby tipped his head slightly and spoke laconically. "This is the best and easiest part of the deal for fellows like you and me, Frank. So far so good. But this outfit will be done loading just about dark. Then the roof comes off and the fun starts. Wild men, fresh off a tough drive trail, wages burning in their pockets—whisky and cards and dance-hall girls. Yeah—you and me—we're due to start earning our pay."

Frank Allard shrugged. "Any rules that your experience has found to be good?"

"Just a realization that they've got a right to a reasonable run for their money. If we can handle things so they get the first edge out of their systems without running too hog-wild, then we'll have done a pretty good job. Most of them won't be too hard to handle, but there's nearly always one or two who fancy themselves as being more than tough. And they're the buckos we'll have to watch real close."

A stocky man in store clothes came down along the

railroad track from the station house. His lone concession to the mode of the country being a big Stetson hat tipped over one eye. He lifted a careless hand to Mosby as he passed. "Marshal, how are you?"

"Who's that fellow?" Allard asked when the man was out of earshot.

"Jack Pollock. Cattle buyer for Lord & McKeever. Shrewd *hombre* in a cattle deal, but a square enough man. Plays a damn good hand of stud poker, too."

Allard stared after the cattle buyer, thoughts hidden behind narrowed eyes. According to what Gil Paxton had told him, Pollock was the man who had bought the herd from Jim Creightly. Which made a talk with Pollock in order when the opportunity offered.

The day ran its course, the tumult at the loading pens never slackening for a moment until just before dark, the last critter was herded into the last car and the train made up to go lumbering and clacking away to the east, its departing whistle a lonely wail across the wide plain.

Freshly shaven, Frank Allard went down to supper and knew a little start of surprise at seeing Barbara Chancellor at a table with Royce Twitchell. From the twin spots of color burning in the girl's cheeks and young Twitchell's almost open sulkiness, it was plain that neither was enjoying the meal. Allard, catching Barbara's eye, nodded gravely, and went on to a corner table.

At another table two men sat, still in the rough clothes of the long cattle trail they had traveled. One was a man of about sixty, thin and leathery, with deep, cold eyes and a harsh mouth. His companion was considerably younger, swarthy, with a mop of curly black hair and bold eyes, which now and again settled on Barbara Chancellor with a hungry intentness, looks which stirred a wave of irritation in Allard.

Once, Allard caught the fellow's roving glance and held it with a calculated impact. But the trail rider showed only a leering grin and deliberately put his attention back on Barbara once more. A little later Allard knew another start of surprise when the older man got up abruptly and came over to his table.

"Name's Starke," said the man curtly. "Abel Starke. I owned that herd that just went off. See you pack a badge. Now I don't know how far your authority reaches, but here's something I want to lay on the line. Night before last my herd was raided. Came damn near being stampeded plumb to hell and gone. One of my men, riding night hawk, was killed. Me and the rest of the boys were too busy trying to get the herd under control and quieted down again to go after the raiders then. I knew I'd lost some cattle, but I didn't know how many until we made the loading count today. My loss came up as right close to a hundred head."

"That's bad business," said Allard quietly. "I'm sorry to hear about it."

"Somebody is going to be damn well good and sorry," Starke threatened. "I don't take kindly to being rustled to the tune of five head, let alone a hundred. Somebody is going to pay for that and for the killing of Dal Wilkins, too. Now while I'm having my say, I'll add this. Me and my boys expect to get our money's worth while we're in this damn town. If we don't, then we'll take the place plumb apart. Now you know."

A shading of frost showed in Allard's eyes. "Friend, here's something else being laid on the line. I say again I'm sorry to hear about your rustling troubles. But I see no proof that anybody in this town had anything to do with it. Big country hereabouts. Lots of trails in and out. So I suggest that neither you or any of your crew try to take out your mad feelings on this town. Have a good time and the best of luck to you. But no rough stuff. Hear me—no rough stuff! That's out. Do I make myself clear?"

"I don't trust any of you trail-town jingoes. You say

this when you mean that. Mebbe you know who those rustlers were, eh?"

"And maybe you're a liar!" shot back Allard.

The frost in Allard's eyes was suddenly ice. The cattleman's lips pulled thin with anger, and for a moment he stared back. Then he shrugged. "One of these proud buckos, eh? Well, we'll see!"

He turned and went back to his table. Allard resumed his supper, masking the quick anger he'd shown at the cattleman's words and bald inferences behind a taciturn inscrutability. He could understand this fellow Starke's feelings about rustled cattle and the death of one member of his crew, but that still didn't justify the fellow's sweeping, hostile charges. Allard could see that Lee Mosby hadn't exaggerated the ominous possibilities of the night ahead. Things could indeed come up rough!

Starke and his companion finished eating just ahead of Allard. They moved along the dining room with Starke leading the way, a vitriolic man full of the acid of loss. Starke did not stop, but the swarthy one with the curly black hair did. He stopped beside the table where Barbara Chancellor and Royce Twitchell sat. Barbara reddened nervously under the boldness of the rider's eyes, and Royce Twitchell made a show of getting to his feet. The cowboy drove an open hand against Royce's chest, slamming him back into his chair.

"Careful!" came the somewhat guttural warning. "I feed on *hombres* like you. But pretty girls—" and here the fellow showed his leering grin, "I sure do like to look at pretty girls. Sister, what house do you work in?"

Barbara Chancellor went utterly white, while Royce Twitchell again acted as though to get to his feet, yet somehow not quite managing it.

The trail hand laughed huskily and started to make further remarks to Barbara, but at that moment Frank Allard had him by the arm.

"Mister, they keep the animals outside this hotel. On your way!"

The trail hand whirled, twisted clear, and aimed a fist at Allard's face. Allard stepped inside the swinging blow and sank a savage fist under the trail hand's heart. The fellow sagged, gasping. Allard hit him twice more in the same place, left and right. Then he grabbed him and drove him on shambling, rubber legs along the rest of the room, out into the foyer of the hotel, then out the door to the porch beyond, and with a final, twisting throw sent him tumbling to hands and knees in the street beyond.

Abel Starke was standing on the porch steps, in the act of lighting a cheroot. At the explosion of action beside him he froze, match in one hand, cheroot half-lifted to his lips with the other. In the street, still gulping and gasping for breath, the trail hand was making fumbling attempts to reach his gun. Frank Allard's voice rang coldly.

"You want to keep him alive, Starke, do something!"

The cattleman snapped out of his daze. "Forget that gun, Blackie! Forget it, I said!"

Blackie didn't appear to hear him, so, jumping down the steps, Starke twisted the weapon away from him. In the last of dusk's fading light, the trail hand made a hunched-over, thickly cursing blot against the earth.

"Smart!" rapped Allard. "He'd been ready for burying in another couple of seconds."

Allard had his own gun out, couched at his hip. Now he gave it a little wave. "The far end of the street, Starke—that's your territory, you and your crew. Keep this one and the rest down there, if this is the breed of stuff you're paying wages to."

"You'd be setting up a deadline, maybe?" challenged Starke.

"Call it that if you want. Anyhow, it stands!"

Starke said something he'd said before. "We'll see."

After which, he steered the protesting rider off into the early night.

Allard went back into the hotel, where Ben Ripon stood, grave-faced. "I'm sorry this had to happen, Mister Allard. But I had no idea—."

"Not your fault, Ben," assured Allard. "But if you've got a shotgun on the premises, load it, and keep it handy. From now on, people like Blackie don't step inside this door."

The little hotelkeeper nodded. "Not one damn step!"

Barbara Chancellor and Royce Twitchell had come out of the dining room. Barbara was still pale, but the flame of a vast indignation burned in her eyes. Royce Twitchell started tossing some bluster.

"You didn't handle that fellow right in there, Allard. You should have taken a gun and..."

"Didn't see you handling him at all," cut in Allard curtly. "Somehow you just couldn't get out of that chair, could you?" He turned his back on young Twitchell and looked at the girl. "So Lafe Oglevie was right, after all."

Her nerves jangled, Barbara flared. "Are you trying to say it was my fault? How could I guess that that fool—that crude brute...?"

"You couldn't, of course," said Allard gently. "Yet, it was the chance of something like this happening that Lafe Oglevie was thinking of when he said you shouldn't be in town. However, as long as you are here, you stick close to this hotel. Don't you leave it tonight."

"That," she retorted, "sounds like an order."

"That's what it was meant to be—an order."

Allard turned and went out. Royce Twitchell started after him, his glance simmering. "The officious fool! Since he started wearing that tin badge, all he can think of is pushing other people around. It's gone to his head—bad!"

"There, Mr. Twitchell, you're wrong," spoke up Ben Ripon, a little edge showing in the words. "Frank Allard does what he thinks should be done. I admire him, and trust him fully. He is my good friend, and I will listen to nothing against him in my hotel." The little hotel owner turned to Barbara. "I'm sure he was thinking only of what's best for you, Miss Chancellor."

Barbara did not answer. Half-angry, half-subdued, she stared at the door through which Allard had disappeared. She turned then and went into the hotel parlor. Royce Twitchell followed, sulky and scowling.

Out in the street, Frank Allard crossed to the office. Lee Mosby sat inside, just beyond the fringe of a meager cone of light thrown by the lamp.

"Had cause to set up a sort of deadline, Lee," Allard told him. "The idea is to keep that trail crew at the far end of the street."

"How come?" grunted the marshal. "Could be a mite tough to make stand."

Allard explained matters briefly. Mosby stirred angrily. "Damned raw thing on the part of that fellow Blackie. All things considered, you let him off easy. As for Starke, I can understand him being galled by that rustling deal. But why take it out on us? We didn't steal any of his damned cows."

Allard shrugged. "Pawnee is the hub of this stretch of country, and Starke's mad at everybody in it. He'll probably cool off. He got some talk out of his system and that generally helps. Any of this rustling stuff ever happen before?"

"Some, I suppose. Coming up the trail, most of the herds run into trouble of some kind along the way. If it's not rustling, it's a couple of tough rivers to cross, or a stampede breaking in the middle of the night, cattle spooking at the fool things they do. Some trouble is always to be expected. So there you have it, Frank; the life of a cowhand. If it ain't one damn thing, then it's something else."

Allard smiled grimly. "How about the life of a town marshal?"

"Ha!" Mosby grunted again. "Maybe you got something there. Well, seeing I've caught up on my sleep the past couple of days, and considering Mister Abel Starke and his playful boys, I'm making it a night with you. Two of us, traveling around together may act as a damper on some of the gayer spirits."

"Not necessary," said Allard gruffly. "But I appreciate the thought."

A spur jangled outside and a cowhand appeared in the doorway. He was a lean, brown young fellow, with an intriguing grin that was partly friendly, partly challenging.

"Heard some talk that there was a deadline set up at this end of town," he said. "Now I ain't aimin' to argue that point with anybody. But I need some new clothes. What I got wasn't much when I started up the trail, and the way things stand right now I'm liable to come unshucked any minute. The store, they tell me, is up this end of town. What's a feller to do about it?" He paused, then added, "Name's Sam Lorry. I'm Slash S, same as Blackie Burke. But I ain't his breed nohow."

Allard studied this straight-eyed, ragged rider, then smiled. "Trot right along and get your clothes. That deadline isn't against any legitimate business. And you do look kind of frayed around the edges, for a fact."

Sam Lorry's grin widened. "Ain't I, though? Now I don't pose as no dude, but I do like to look at least halfway civilized." He turned to go, then paused, his grin fading. "You watch Blackie Burke. He's pretty low stuff and no damn good. So you keep an eye on him."

He went away then, spurs tinkling. Lee Mosby sighed. "Now if all these trail riders were as friendly and harmless as that cub, we wouldn't have a thing to worry about, Frank."

They sat for a while and smoked, ears cocked to the rising tempo of life down-street. Mosby had another thought. "Wonder what Gil Paxton will think of this deadline idea? He may figure it will shut him off from business."

"I'll go explain matters to him," Allard said.

He went out and along to the store. It was one of spring's deep dark nights when the light that the stars gave out was smothered by a velvety blackness before it could reach the earth. The air was chilling and a slow drift of it coming down from the Bench and from the Vestal Hills beyond gave promise of perhaps a touch of late season frost.

A stir on the porch resolved itself into Gil Paxton and Con Waters. They too were listening to the voice of the town. "Could be a rough night ahead, Frank," observed Paxton.

"Just so," Allard agreed. He went on to explain the deadline idea. "Doesn't apply to anybody with legitimate business of course."

"Quite all right," Paxton approved. "Legitimate business is the only kind Con and me are interested in. Pinto Jardene and his kind can have the rest."

"Already sent you one customer," Allard observed. "Decent looking kid."

"He's inside now," Paxton said. "Nell's waiting on him."

Allard moved to the door and looked in. Sam Lorry stood at the counter, his pile of purchases in front of him. Across the counter was Nell Kane. She was smiling at some remark the young cowhand had made. The pair seemed quite oblivious to everything around them.

Allard backed away. As he did so, a wild, pealing yell sounded somewhere down by the Palace. Behind the yell was whisky, anger, and a certain loosening savagery. "This way, Slash S—this way!"

"Now it starts," said Allard. He went off at a run.

Gil Paxton spat past the edge of the porch. "Yeah," he said harshly, "now it starts. Those damn trail herds and what they bring with them, Con. They turn our town into a jungle full of crazy animals."

He turned abruptly and went into the store. Nell Kane was laughing softly now, her eyes shining and no trace at all of the old sullenness about her. Sam Lorry was matching her, smile for smile. Gil Paxton spoke bruskly.

"I'll finish with things in here, Nell. You better get upstairs."

The merriment on the girl's face died and she moved toward the stairs reluctantly. At the foot of them she paused, showing a flash of defiance as she gave Sam Lorry a last direct look. "Good night, cowboy," she said. Then, as she climbed the stairs, the old sullenness was back and settled about her mouth once more.

Sam Lorry, startled and a trifle bewildered, gathered up his purchases and moved toward the door. He tried to get his cheerful grin working again, but it wouldn't shape up. For Gil Paxton's lips were compressed and in his attitude there was no friendliness at all. Sam Lorry went out, spurs dragging.

Lee Mosby had already reached the trouble spot when Frank Allard came up. There was a knot of riders pushing and arguing about the door of the Palace, and Allard could hear Mosby's voice above the rest.

"Break it up, boys—break it up!"

"Hell with you," came a snarling answer. "No damn barroom bouncer can manhandle a friend of mine and get away with it!"

"Break it up, he says," bawled another of the crowd. "All right... Let's break up the whole damn joint! Come on Slash S! This way, boys—this way!"

There was a rush for the door. Lee Mosby managed to get there first, and he braced himself to hold back the pressure. Frank Allard drove into the crush, fighting his way to Mosby's side. A swinging fist, seemingly coming from nowhere, smashed into his mouth, and the slime of blood began to dribble down his chin. Anger, wicked and cold, erupted in him. He bent forward, driving through with lunging shoulders. He caught up men and flung them aside. A cursing figure in front of him bounced another fist off his face, and Allard clubbed the man aside with the point of a slicing elbow. Finally reaching Mosby, Allard swung around beside him to face the crowd.

New arrivals to the pack, brought in from other dives by the war cry of the outfit, added weight that Allard and Mosby couldn't stem. They were pushed back through the doorway and swept aside.

A yelling, scar-faced rider picked up a chair and threw it at the long bar mirror. A bartender caught the chair in midair and the rider, cursing, tried to vault the bar to follow up his wild will to destroy. Frank Allard caught him by the collar, hauled him back, and threw him spinning.

At the far end of the room several dance-hall girls were huddled fearfully. Pinto Jardene was there, too, rapping orders to three burly bouncers who were armed with bung starters. The three moved forward to give battle to the mob. For a short moment there was just the slightest pause as the two forces measured each other. Frank Allard, with Lee Mosby close beside him, moved into the gap.

"This thing stops right here!" yelled Allard harshly. "Else somebody gets hurt!"

The scar-faced rider came up off the floor. "You're the one due to get hurt, by God!" And he went at Allard in a diving lunge. Allard slithered a half-stride to one side and smashed a fist wickedly home. The scar-faced one hit the floor again, and this time he didn't get up. Another came darting in at Allard from the side. Blackie Burke it was, aiming to catch Allard off guard. Lee Mosby took care of the swart, black-haired Burke, belting him down with an overhand swing.

"If some damn fool drags a gun, there'll be hell to pay, Frank," panted Mosby hoarsely.

It was the one thing Frank Allard was mainly afraid of. If a gun went off now, this thing could turn into a bloody shambles. And there was no telling when some whisky-crazed rider might start it.

Allard had nothing personal against any of these riders, except perhaps Blackie Burke, because of the fellow's crude and foul behavior earlier in the hotel dining room. He knew the type. He had ridden with many of the same in his time. Sober, and under usual circumstances, most of them were not a bad sort at all. But conditions, plus the release from the long abstinence of the trail could set them off.

Nor was he overly concerned about any damage that might come to Pinto Jardene's establishment. That, in fact, was the least of it. But he was now wearing a badge that subscribed to law and order, and while he carried it, he would make it stand for just that.

Along the far wall a thin, sardonic figure edged into view. It was Abel Starke, boss of these men. His harsh mouth was pulled into a half-smile of anticipation, and he showed no inkling of desire to head this ruckus off. In several long strides, Allard was over beside him.

"They belong to you," Allard rapped. "Call a halt. Should things go any further or get any worse, you'll get more than your share of misery. You heard me—call them off!"

Starke's grin became a taunt. "I told you—."

Allard caught Starke by the shoulder, dug rough fingers deep. "Right now I'm doing the telling. Call them off...!"

Starke writhed under the digging hurt of Allard's grip and the taunt on his lips became a grimace of pain. Under the bleak chill in Allard's eyes the cattleman's glance shifted and he lifted a nasal shout. "That's enough, boys—that's enough. Back away!"

They were still undecided, less than half-willing to listen. But the order from the man who paid their wages offered an opening of which Lee Mosby was quick to take advantage. He put a little more pressure on them, though speaking almost mildly.

"You heard that, boys. It's your boss talking. All you want is a little fun, but you can't find it this way. The night's still young. Scatter out and spend your money."

The wildness began to run out of them; the first flush of mob spirit faded. They began to shift and mutter in indecision. Some at the rear, pulled from other halls of pleasure by that first rallying call, now drifted out into the night again and back to their favored deadfall. As swiftly as it had peaked, the danger in this affair was past.

"Better," Frank Allard told Abel Starke. "A lot better. But I don't want to have to tell you again. Save the rough stuff for those who raided your herd, if you can come up with them. But get rid, finally and for all, of taking it out on this town!"

Starke did not answer. He went out, his men drifting after him. The scar-faced rider and the black-haired Burke were the last to leave. The scar-faced one was sullen and subdued, but Blackie Burke laid a poisonous, hating glance on Allard, together with a gutturally hoarse threat.

"The third chance will be my turn," he promised.

Allard did not answer, merely watched him levelly until the doors had swung closed behind the swarthy one's back.

Lee Mosby grinned crookedly at Allard. "Now that was a close one, Frank. It could have gone bad."

There was a swelling under Mosby's left eye, where someone's fist had landed during the melee at the doorway. Allard, feeling his bruised mouth, nodded. "More and more I like your style, friend. The drinks are on me."

They moved up to the bar. Pinto Jardene came up beside them. His face was impassive, his eyes unreadable. To the bartender he said, "It's on the house, Chet."

"No!" rapped Allard curtly. "Lee and I didn't quiet that crowd down just as a favor to you, Jardene. We did it because it was part of our job. I'm buying this drink."

Jardene stared at him, shrugged, and turned away. Allard stopped him now with further words.

"I don't know exactly what started this ruckus, but I did hear something about one of your bouncers manhandling a rider. Maybe that was justified, maybe it wasn't. But in any case, when those men come in here to spend their money, just remember that they're entitled to a square shake. See that they get it. Lee, here's looking at you!"

They had their drinks and went out.

Pinto Jardene went into the back room and closed the door behind him. Royce Twitchell and his father were at the poker table, chips in front of them. Jardene took the third chair, but showed little inclination to go on with the game.

"What happened in there?" Haley Twitchell asked. "By the racket I thought a real brawl was breaking. What quieted it so sudden?"

Pinto Jardene's eyes took on a hard, shiny glint. "Allard, damn him! Oh, he saved me money, all right. That Slash S gang was set to break things up proper. But this fellow Allard is getting increasingly in the way, and now he's taking that fool Mosby with him. I'm going to send for Ned Fargo."

Haley Twitchell rolled his cigar across his tobacco-stained lips. "Isn't Ned rather busy right about now, Pinto?"

Jardene shrugged. "He should have the big part of the chore pretty well taken care of by this time. Anyhow, I want a report from him."

"How about Harry Shelline?" Royce Twitchell asked.

"He'll come in with Ned Fargo," Jardene said.

Haley Twitchell leaned back, scratched a match to freshen his cigar, then sucked moistly at it. "Wonder if that's wise? No use baiting this Allard character too much right now. Make no mistake about it, Pinto— that man is a tough customer. He could be the rock we smash up on."

Pinto Jardene did not appear to be listening, instead following out a line of reasoning of his own behind pinched eyes. "The time," he said musingly, "has come to force the betting. If Ned and his boys have done as good a job on that other herd coming up the trail as they did on the Slash S, then we'll have a handful of top cards. And if we play those cards right, there's a mighty fat pot to pick up. It's a hand we've been building toward for a long time."

Haley Twitchell stirred with a vague uneasiness. "May not be a simple chore to bring this Abel Starke and his outfit together with that other trail crowd. There's nothing more independent than a trail herd crew."

Jardene smiled thinly. "Common loss makes for common purpose. You let me handle Starke and that other outfit. When I put the fat bait in front of them, they'll be chomping at the bit. Not getting cold feet, are you?"

Haley Twitchell stirred again. "It's a big plan with lots of possibilities, all right," he admitted. "But frankly, it looked better the first time we discussed it."

"Why should it?" Jardene demanded.

"Allard," said Haley Twitchell. "Frank Allard."

Pinto Jardene made a hard, cutting motion with his right hand. "I'll take care of Allard. Before I'm done with him he'll be cut down to size. For that matter I don't see that he's too strong in the main picture."

"Well, I do," Haley Twitchell said bluntly. "He's on good terms now with Lafe Oglevie and the rest of the C Cross. Also, he and the Chancellor girl seem to be hitting it off pretty well. Should he pitch in on their side, just how do you propose to handle him? So far you haven't had much luck."

Pinto Jardene's eyes burned. "He's only one man. And once he's dead, he's nothing. I may give the nod to Harry Shelline—he's hungry for a try at Allard's hide. And if Shelline isn't good enough, there's always Ned Fargo. Yeah, I'll take care of Mister Frank Allard!"

CHAPTER SEVEN

FRANK ALLARD stood on the edge of the hotel porch, where a shaft of morning sunlight could strike him. He lipped an after breakfast cigar a little gingerly as a result of last night's fracas in the Palace barroom. His glance searched the street and found it pleasurably peaceful in comparison to what it had been when the wilder spirits had been on their trouble hunt. But that affair in the Palace, together with several lesser brawls in some of the other deadfalls had left their bruises, some physical, some mental. There was a lingering drag of tension around his lean jaw.

Barbara Chancellor came out on the porch, dressed for riding, and pulling on a pair of worn, deep-cuffed buckskin gauntlets. Despite the soberness of her expression she looked fresh and fine, and Allard, after tipping his head in greeting, told her so. She colored slightly as she paused beside him and had her look at the town, and her expressive lips twisted in a grimace of disgust.

"It makes me think of a drunk sleeping off a whisky debauch," she said abruptly.

"Doesn't take much mud to discolor a stream of clear water," Allard said gravely. "But in a little time that passes and the stream runs clear again."

She threw him a covert glance, marking the bruised condition of his lips, aware of his rangy ruggedness and the cool, deep fire in his eyes.

"I heard about that affair in the Palace. Why did you stop it? Why didn't you let that trail crew go ahead and smash the place up? It would have been a blessing, not a loss."

He shook his head. "No, that wouldn't have been right, either. The law can't play favorites. Once it starts that, it's no longer the law. Even such as Pinto Jardene is entitled to a fair shake. Besides, if that thing had been allowed to spread, somebody might have been hurt bad. Or it could have spread to more respectable places in town, like Ben Ripon's hotel."

She colored again, remembering the evening before and the crass and insulting advances offered her by Blackie Burke in the hotel dining room.

"Just why," she demanded fiercely, "do men have to act as they do? They're supposed to be creatures of the higher intelligence, not animals. Yet at times they are worse than animals. Whisky, cards, those—those dance-hall women...They fight, pound one another like wild brutes. They shoot, kill...And then, when they sober up, they try to walk with pride and dignity. I—I just don't understand it!"

Allard took a long pull at his cigar, and let the pale smoke sift from his lips to curl upward past his lean head. "Perhaps," he defended quietly, "they don't exactly understand it themselves. Maybe it's just that the

Lord made them that way. And the things you mention could be a safety valve for the stored-up energy accumulated during the long, hard chore of bringing a herd up the trail, with all its tough, tiresome miseries and dangers. And when that chore is finished, such men just have to bust loose some way. Then too, there could be other reasons."

He paused for another drag at his cigar. "With some it could be a means of forgetting, or trying to forget some thwarted ambition, or blasted hope, or smashed-up ideal. With some it could be a black specter of memory behind them and nothing but a gray hopelessness ahead. And so, for a little time, they would forget."

"Did you feel that way toward them last night during that brawl in the Palace?" demanded Barbara.

He smiled faintly. "Not exactly at that moment, perhaps. When some bucko cowhand is doing his damndest best to beat your face in, why then you haven't time to do anything else but beat him to the punch if you can. But after it's over with and matters have cooled down, why then you try to give him the benefit of the doubt. He's probably feeling the same way about you."

Frowning, she stared straight ahead, as though trying to understand this somewhat puzzling masculine viewpoint. "Supposing, during that trouble, one of those trail hands had pulled a gun on you—what would you have done then?"

"Done my best to beat him to the shot, of course." A thread of curtness crept into Allard's tone. "That's fundamental, that a man should strive to go on living, even if he has to kill to do it. Nature wrote that law and gave it to all her creatures."

"And," persisted Barbara, "after you had lived and the other man had died, you'd have known regret?"

"To a degree, yes. That would depend, of course, on just what type the other man was. If he was an average sort, neither all good nor all bad, gone shooting wild because of an overload of whisky, then there would certainly be regret. On the other hand, if he was completely no good, never had been and never would be, then the feeling would be different. It's a pretty difficult thing to be wholly one way or the other. You can't see all things as being all white or all black, as there are a lot of varying shades of gray in between."

She studied him a little gravely, and, meeting the glance, Allard gave her that brief smile again. "It's much too fine a morning to waste in going over last night's shadows and taking them apart. The way you pulled on those gloves suggests you might be going somewhere."

"Which I am," she declared. "I'm going to relieve your mind and Lafe Oglevie's, too. I'm going home."

"Now there's a fine idea," exclaimed Allard approvingly. "Not that we want to get rid of you, understand. But until the town really quiets down again, home is the right place for you."

He walked along the street with her to Con Waters' stable, and they waited there while Con went in after her horse.

"I'm mightily tempted to get my roan and ride along with you," Allard said. "But that wouldn't be fair to Lee Mosby. He stood the night shift with me, so I can't let him down today."

"Ben Ripon says that Mosby surprises him," Barbara observed. "That Mosby seems like a changed man. And that, for a change, he carries his badge as though it really means something."

"Lee's all right," Allard said. "He's found there's more to himself than he realized."

The girl threw a quick, slanting glance up at the rangy, solid man beside her. "Strength," she murmured, "so it has been said, can give off strength."

Con Waters came out with her horse, and Barbara, swinging up, went into her saddle with her sure, easy grace. She thanked Con Waters, gave Allard a quick, warming smile, and rode away.

Con and Allard watched her until she made the turn out of town into the Bench road. Then Con turned and looked at Allard. "A little excitement last night."

Allard shrugged. "Some. Mostly noise."

Con dropped a hand on Allard's arm briefly before turning away. "Good man," he murmured.

Allard sauntered over to Gil Paxton's store where Sam Lorry, the young Slash S rider, sat on the edge of the porch. Allard showed him a small grin. "You look like a different man, Sam."

Sam Lorry nodded, his brown young face serious. "I am, in more ways than one. Tell me, what's the chances for a young feller in this country? Like settling down, working hard, and getting somewhere?" He twisted up a smoke while he spoke. "I like this country, I surely do."

Allard, remembering the rapt way in which young Sam and Nell Kane had faced each other across the store counter last evening, showed that small grin again. "Just the country, Sam?"

Sam looked up, his eyes serious and steady. "And some of the people in it," he admitted frankly. "I'm hoping they'll like me."

Allard sat down beside him. "Maybe she does, Sam."

Under his heavy weather tan the young puncher colored slightly. "She's swell," he said softly. "First girl I ever met up with who made me start realizing there could be a lot more to life than just shaggin' up and down the trail for forty and found. Ain't no future for a man in that." A trifle ruefully, he added, "That father of hers ain't what you'd call overly friendly, though."

Allard scratched a match and freshened his cigar. "You figure him to butter you all over the first time he sets eyes on you?"

"No, of course not. But shucks, he didn't have to look at me like I was something crawling on its belly instead of a man walking on two feet. That sure took the shine off what had been a few mighty big minutes for me."

Allard played with silent thoughts for a time. He liked this serious, straightforward kid. There was none of the dullness of a wild night in Sam's eyes, but instead a clear and settled honesty. Sam Lorry hadn't spent the night in some dive, but instead had been out in his soogan roll under the clean stars, dreaming his great young dreams.

Allard had known such dreams himself at one time. Then they had dulled and turned gray and shapeless, with no great meaning anymore. Laura had been her name, and he had thought that she was very fine and beautiful in all ways. And had found out abruptly that she was neither. So he had carried bitterness for a considerable time until the action and purpose of a strong man's life had scrubbed out the memory until it neither hurt or mattered anymore. Instead it had merely left him with the conviction that he would never unarmor his feelings again for such a going-over. So far he'd managed to hold onto that conviction pretty well. But....

His glance lifted to the higher sweep of the Bench road, in time to glimpse a slender, straight-backed rider just topping the crest and then moving on out of sight. And of a sudden he knew a feeling of kinship with this kid beside him, along with the desire to give the kid a break in understanding.

"Gil Paxton isn't Nell Kane's father, Sam. He took her in and gave her a home when she was about fourteen. This was after her real father had been lynched for stealing cattle."

Sam Lorry was jolted. Then his brown young jaw firmed and he flared defensively. "What her father was is no fault of hers. And it don't make any difference to me. Would it to you?"

"No, it wouldn't," admitted Allard quietly. "But that is something you'd have to take her away from and make her forget, and never mention to her, ever!"

"Think I'd want to hurt her?" demanded young Sam vehemently.

Allard smiled gravely. "Right now you're trying to ride a trail you haven't even come to, Sam. A thing like this has to be given a little time. And when Starke heads back for his home range, what'll he say if you don't go with him?"

"What can he say? I've more than earned every dollar Abel Starke ever paid me. I don't owe him anything, and I'm my own man."

Allard stood up. "Nobody can ever hold it against you for trying, son."

There was a certain awkwardness, but also a strong eagerness in young Sam's next words. "You think you might be able to put in a good boost for me, Mister Allard?"

"Do my best, Sam."

Allard went back to the hotel, for there was a man sitting on the hotel porch in a round-backed chair, to whom he wanted to talk. This was Jack Pollock, cattle buyer. Pollock threw him an inquiring glance as he pulled up another chair and settled into it.

"Know who you are," said Allard quietly. "Me, I'm Frank Allard. Mind if I ask you a few questions?"

Pollock glanced at Allard's badge, then showed a dry humor. "Fly to it. Offhand though, I can't think of any law I've broken lately."

Allard smiled faintly. "Nothing like that. But you might be able to give me a line on somebody who did."

Pollock's expression suggested a hard-headed shrewdness, but also a definite integrity of character as Allard went on. "I'm going to ask you to keep this in confidence. If that suits you, I'll say the rest."

Jack Pollock shrugged. "I've batted around cattle country enough to know that the safest thing any man can do is keep his mouth shut. I've known of more than one man who got killed because he opened his at the wrong time and place. That answer you?"

111

Allard nodded. "This has to do with a man who was killed. Right in this town. You bought a herd from him. Jim Creightly was his name."

Pollock straightened, his expression turning sober. "Right on every count. What about it?"

"Jim Creightly was my partner," explained Allard slowly. "And I'd give a lot to come up with the man who shot him in the back. That's why I wanted to speak with you and see if you had any ideas you'd care to voice?"

Pollock settled back in his chair. "If you mean about who pulled that dirty trick, then no, I've not the slightest idea. I'll say this, though. When I heard of Creightly being killed it sure set me back, because I liked the man. He played square with me, I played square with him. You know, Allard—when it comes to buying cattle, a man learns as much about humans as he does about stock. For instance, he learns that there are some he can trust and some that he can't. Take a deal of this sort. You buy a herd of say five hundred head or more. The cars are waiting and the demurrage is a ghost always at your elbow that can bite a big chunk out of your legitimate profit on the deal. Also, no beef critter puts on extra weight while fretting around in a shipping pen. So time means money."

"Know what you mean," Allard said.

"So it figures down that you don't have time to look over every critter too carefully," went on Pollock. "Which means that to a degree, you got to take the word of the man you're buying from that he's not trying to slip something over on you. Sometimes that word isn't worth a damn. With Jim Creightly it was. When that shipment reached the yards at Kansas City, it shaped up exactly as he said it would be. He didn't try to slip a single off-condition critter through on me. I can respect the memory of a man like that. So you can believe me when I say that if I had any idea at all of who did for him, and why, I'd be only too glad to speak up. But I haven't."

Allard pursed his lips, stared straight ahead. "Was afraid it would be that way. But I had to ask. If I could only figure a motive, I might get somewhere. More than anything else, that's what I had in mind when I asked you about ideas."

"I've thought some about it, of course," Pollack admitted. "Along this line. I paid Creightly a considerable chunk of money for that herd. In gold. The deal was bound to become common knowledge about town, so it could have been that somebody figured on knocking Creightly off to get that money. In other words—robbery. Which seemed to me as likely a motive as any."

"Considered that myself," Allard said. "Anyway, thanks—I appreciate what you've told me."

The day ran along and around the middle of the afternoon, Frank Allard sauntered into the store and found Gil Paxton alone. By his expression, the storekeeper was out of sorts. Allard casually remarked on the fact.

"Something under the saddle blanket that's galling you, Gil?"

Paxton started to shake his head, then answered testily. "These damned, shiftless, drifting cowpokes! If they don't quit hanging around here, ogling Nell every time she shows her face, I'm liable to start getting rough. Thought you'd set up a deadline? How about making it stick?"

Allard perched on the counter, drummed his heels. "Anyone in particular you're aiming at, Gil?"

"Yeah," snapped Paxton. "Couple of them. There was one in here just a little bit ago. Cocky devil. Swarthy, with a lot of curly, black hair. Nell was helping me stock up some shelves. That fellow leered at her like she was some floozy from the lowest dive in town. I asked him what his damn business was and he had the gall to say that he'd heard that a pretty girl lived here

113

at the store and that he wanted to have a look at her. I told him to get the hell out, and quick, or I'd unload a shotgun into him. He laughed at me, but he left, saying he'd probably be back for another look. Well, if he shows again, he'll get just what I promised him!"

Frank Allard made a silent note to look up one Blackie Burke and lay a few cold facts on the line. Aloud he said, "Doubt he'll bother again, Gil. Wouldn't let it worry me."

"He ain't the only one," Paxton fumed. "There's also that young buck who was in here last night buying an outfit of clothes. I shouldn't have let Nell wait on him, I guess. Now he's been hanging around here all morning, mooning like a calf-eyed puppy. Hell of it is, Nell seems all of a dither about him."

"Well," Allard drawled, "what's so strange about that? Nell's young and pretty. And that kid puncher, Sam Lorry, he shapes up as a decent, clean-cut sort. Life's like that, Gil. Young folks meet up and are attracted to each other."

Paxton waved an impatient hand. "No run-over-at-the-heels cowpoke is going to hang around Nell. I'll bust his back if he tries!"

Allard kept up his mildly curious pose. "Just what have you got figured out for Nell's future, anyhow, if it's any of my business?"

"Well, it ain't your business," said Paxton shortly. "So let's drop it!"

Allard's eyes pinched down a trifle and his tone went crisp. "I'm saying a few things, first. Did it ever strike you that hanging around this store and your living quarters up above, day in and day out, can get mighty lonely and monotonous to a girl like Nell? Oh, a good enough sort of an existence for you, maybe, as you're at the age in life when you're concerned with little else than your business and a reasonably comfortable routine of living. But a younger spirit could know a natural

114

yearning for something far bigger and brighter than that."

"Nell's got nothing to kick about," retorted Paxton. "I've been good to that girl. I've treated her right."

"True, to a point." Allard nodded. "You've fed and clothed and sheltered her, and that's all to your eternal credit. But, man—she's no longer the kid she was when you took her in. Nell's a young woman now, with the forces of nature running strong in her. She wants her man, a home of her own, her slice of life. And she's got a right to all that. Gil, it's a current that not you or anybody else can stand in front of forever. You'd be damned pig-headed and selfish if you tried. Think it over."

"I know my business and I'll tend to it," growled Paxton harshly. "Suppose you tend to yours!"

Allard slid off the counter, looked the storekeeper up and down. "You can be a stubborn fool, can't you, Gil? Keep on as you're doing and you could make the wrong kind of woman out of Nell Kane. Seems you haven't got sense enough to realize that."

Allard went out. Paxton stared after the broad lift of those tall departing shoulders, and a strange, almost fanatical light began to burn in his eyes.

From the store, Allard went back to the hotel and to his room. He pulled off his boots and stretched out on the bed, hands behind his head as he stared somberly up at the ceiling. There was a restlessness taking hold in him and the beginnings of a gnawing dissatisfaction with things as he was now living them. He could see that this job he'd taken over would not last too long. Not because of what others might have to say about it, but because of his own growing distaste.

There was within him a deep well of strength and energy that had, in the past, found an outlet in hard work and plenty of activity on the freedom of an open range. He knew he could not long stand this lying around, spending virtually all of his waking hours within the confines of this town of Pawnee, with its few virtues and its many vices, with its cheap politics and its grudges and its narrowness of outlook.

He recalled his talk with Gil Paxton, just concluded. There, he mused, was a perfect example of what too long a town existence could do to a man. A man grooved to a certain tempo of colorless living and, it seemed, perfectly content to go on with it for all the rest of his days. Never knowing some of life's deepest physical trials, like raw hunger or cold or thirst or sodden fatigue, but never knowing the great moments, either. Like the thrill of life's strong tide in the sweet lift of dawn, with another day of freeness in the saddle waiting just ahead. And these were the things that made life worth living, these high moments and low, this change and challenge and variety.

For the wealth of a man's days was not something he could measure only in dollar value; it was what he wrung from those days in the pure process of living, and in what great dreams he had and how far they carried him.

These, it seemed, were the things that Gil Paxton apparently could not understand, and why he was blind to the yearnings of a girl like Nell Kane. None of his, Frank Allard's business, was what Gil Paxton had said. Allard stirred a little. Maybe so and maybe not...

Came a knock at the door and it was Ben Ripon who entered. The little hotelkeeper was solemnly serious as he squared himself in front of Allard and spoke with slow care. "Got something on my mind that won't let me rest until I get rid of it. You mind?"

Allard sat up, found a cigar, and set it going. "Of course not, Ben. I don't mind. Let's have it."

Ben Ripon took a chair, sort of crouched there, his hands palm to palm as he pressed them between his knees. His glance held steadily on Allard.

"I didn't mean to listen in. But there was a window open and I was just inside it, readin' a stockman's journal. Then you started talkin' to Jack Pollock and while you kept your voice pretty low, I guess I heard most of it. I didn't do it on purpose. I just did, if you get what I mean." This little man, Ben Ripon, was apologetic but determined.

Frank Allard held out his cigar, stared at it, then flicked the new tip of ash aside.

"I understand how that could be, Ben. Go on."

Ripon nodded. "Heard you mention Jim Creightly. Heard you say he'd been your partner. Heard you say you'd like to come up with the man who killed him."

Ben Ripon went silent, blinking. Frank Allard leaned forward, his eyes showing a sharpening light. "Maybe you know something about that, Ben?"

"Not for sure," answered the hotelkeeper slowly. "Mebbe I don't know anythin' about it. And that's the hell of it. Now if I knew somethin' for dead certain, one way or the other, why that'd be that, and I could quit wonderin' and frettin' about it."

"Anything you can tell me will help, Ben. And I'm listening."

"Well, here's one thing. There's the general story of the killin' that's gone round what most folks figger the way it was. And among others there was three of us who heard the shot, Gil Paxton, Con Waters, and me. But there was somethin' else I didn't hear."

Frank Allard was leaning forward, intent on every word. "What was it you didn't hear, Ben?"

"Why, I didn't hear anybody runnin' down the street after the shot...Gil Paxton, he claims he heard somebody runnin' away, down-street. If that had been so, then I'd sure of heard them, too, for anybody runnin' down-street from the store, they'd have to come past this hotel. But I didn't hear nobody. The street was plumb empty except for Gil and Con up there with a lantern, bending over Jim Creightly."

Frank Allard was still, the mask of taciturn remoteness settling across his face. Ben Ripon unclasped his hands, rubbed them back and forth on his trouser legs, then clasped them again.

"Where were you when you heard the shot, Ben?" asked Allard.

"Tidyin' up around the register desk."

"And you ran out onto the porch just as soon as you heard the shot?"

"That's it."

"How long would you say it was between the time you heard the shot and until you were out on the porch?"

"How long would it take a man to scamper less'n fifty feet? That would be it."

Allard was still again, sunk in brooding thought. He fixed Ben Ripon with another direct glance.

"What you're driving at is that there's more to the story behind the killing of Jim Creightly than's been told. Is that it?"

The hotelkeeper bobbed a vigorous head. "That's the point that keeps me all twisted up. Because me—I just can't figger why Gil Paxton would say there was somebody runnin' down the street when there sure enough wasn't."

Allard's cigar had gone out. He lit it again, squinting through the smoke. "I've reason to believe that Gil Paxton is an honest man, Ben."

"Hell, yes—I know he is," exclaimed Ripon. "Gil wouldn't cheat you out of a nickel on any account. You owe him a dime, he wants it. He owes you one, he'll pay you if it kills him. But bein' honest that way wouldn't necessarily keep a man from coverin' up for somebody else in another way. There's plenty of angles to human nature and some of 'em are sure damn queer ones."

The hotelkeeper got to his feet and moved toward the door. "I reckon I can count on you keepin' this to yourself, Mister Allard?"

"Of course," Allard assured him. "Just one more

question, Ben. Have you got any idea who Gil Paxton would be covering up for, if that's the way it is?"

The little man shook his head. "Not a single idea. But I just got to admit to a mighty strong feelin' somehow that Gil Paxton ain't tellin' all he knows about the killin' of Jim Creightly."

Left alone, Frank Allard lay back on his bed again in brooding thought. And the more he thought, the darker his mood became and the less he was sure of anything.

The black mood stayed with him the balance of the day and even through supper and still had hold of him when he stepped out into the night's first darkness. He did not go over to the office, but instead turned along the street toward the Palace and past it, moving on toward the far west end of town.

There had always been somewhat of a solitary streak in his makeup, and his present mood deepened this until right now he had no wish to talk to Lee Mosby or anyone else. He simply knew a nagging restlessness which only movement could assuage.

Window and door shot yellow lances of light into the dark. The piano in the Palace was thumping and the high, brassy laughter of some dance-hall girl carried past it. A small group of cowhands, spur chains clashing, moved along the far side of the street, arguing fitfully among themselves over little of any consequence.

He went the full length of the street, where the town frittered out in a last fringe of scattered shanties. Beyond these outskirts lay just the plain, running away into the limitless dark. He stood there for a time, his back to town, facing the world's emptiness and its big silence, drawing on its peace and its strength. He stayed so until he'd finished his after supper cigar. Then he headed slowly back, a strange hate for this town crawling up in him like some dark venom.

The night life of the town was beginning to move

but was still orderly. He hoped it would stay that way but concluded it probably wouldn't. When the liquor took hold and began to burn, ran his cynical thought, the wilder spirits of the night would start whooping it up. Well, he decided grimly, they'd better not run too wild, as they would get little gentle handling on his part, the way he felt just now.

The shadowy bulk of the Palace loomed ahead, its higher part lifting black against the stars, while its lights glared garishly lower down. The piano was still thumping as the Palace welcomed business. The Palace, hub of this town's wickedness, with its back room and its tawdry secrets.

Allard wondered what the Palace might know about Jim Creightly's murder. Not that it cared a damn, that was certain. But it probably knew something, all right. And whatever it might be, there was, he realized, little if any chance of getting such information out of the place. Such dives as the Palace kept their secrets well.

He came even with the first corner of the place, where shadow lay black and heavy. And it was from this darkened angle that the flame of a gun and the hard, heavy voice of it lashed out at him, while the shock of the bullet sent him staggering.

He was spinning, clawing for his own weapon, when still another voice—this time a human one—struck out also, cold and toneless. The voice of Harry Shelline, tinhorn gambler and killer.

"Takes more than words, Allard, to run me out of town—and make it stick!"

Then the gun flamed again.

CHAPTER EIGHT

FRANK ALLARD was on his knees. He couldn't remember going down that far, nor could he figure how he got there. He knew only that a savagely heavy blow had struck him over the heart, knocking him off balance, flooding him with a gasping numbness. This he knew, and also that now his own gun was in his fist and that it was bucking in recoil, slamming its flame and thunder through the night.

He had no visible target. He had only the echo of a cold, relentless voice and illusory blobs of gun flame, making the night's blackness open and close, open and close. These were the things that he shot at, the echo of a voice and the flame of a snarling gun.

This was such a time when a man struck back at danger through pure instinct alone. There was no time for ordered thought or calculated purpose, no time for anything but to throw shot after shot until the gun in his hand clicked empty and useless.

Now that other gun was still, also, as was the voice that had been behind it. Now there was only a single long, whistling sigh, and after that the numbed silence of a shocked and waiting night.

But the hard, thudding rumble of the guns that had gone before had reached the ears of men all along the street, so now came the shouts of men, a wondering curse or two, and the pound of running feet, all things that Frank Allard heard but dimly and knew no concern about. For he was hunched over, numbed and shaken and sick. A great agony lay all through his chest, and he couldn't get enough air into his lungs.

They came charging up on all sides, wondering anxiety in a voice or two, but for the most part just a raucous morbidity in the others. They pushed and shoved and trampled, and excited questions flew unanswered. One of the gathering crowd stumbled against Allard.

"Here's one!" he yelled. "Must be hit. He's part way down!"

Then it was Lee Mosby's voice, harsh and commanding. "Get back—back away, everybody! I want a look at this."

Mosby dropped a hand on Allard's shoulder, bent over him. "Where you hit, man? What—? God's name— Frank Allard!"

Of a sudden that cold, terrible paralysis of agony in Allard's chest broke and loosened. He was able to breathe again, and he gulped hungrily for air. His heart raced madly and strength began to return. He stumbled to his feet, mumbling thickly.

"It was Shelline, Lee. Over at the corner of the Palace. He was laying for me there and he opened up without warning. His first shot knocked me down. But I'm feeling better now—and I don't understand why..."

Mosby slid an arm around him, steering his uncertain steps toward the hotel. "Somebody locate Doc Sanchez," Mosby yelled. "Send him over to the hotel. Easy, Frank—easy!"

At first the surface of the street seemed like a rolling, undulating sea, but the further he went the steadier things became. Ben Ripon was on the hotel porch, and there was a very real concern in his sharp exclamation.

"Mister Allard! You've been hit?"

"Must be, Ben," Allard answered, his voice stronger. "But I'm feeling quite chipper now, and I tell you I can't understand it. Lee, I can make it all right now. You better go look to Shelline. I think I got lead into him."

"Hell with Shelline!" exploded Mosby. "He don't rate at all. Ben, give a hand."

So they got him to his room and set the lamp alight. Despite the tide of returning strength it felt mighty good to stretch out on the bed. For his heart was still pounding heavily, and the pulse of surging blood was a throbbing rushing in his ears. Allard sighed with a deep relief as he lay back.

There were hurrying steps along the hall, and then Doctor Sanchez came bustling in. He was a round little man with dark, intelligent eyes. "What's this—what's this?" he demanded. "Where's he hit?"

"Don't know, Doc," Mosby answered. "Take a look."

Doc did so, then paused, swearing in soft wonder. "I will be everlastingly damned! See here, Mosby!"

It was Allard's badge of office, torn almost loose from his shirt, hanging now by just a shred of cloth. The metal badge was deeply creased, bent almost double. Along that crease were gray streaks of crushed lead.

"I know better," said Doc Sanchez. "The major training of my life in a science based on an utter and complete realism tells me that such a thing can't happen. Yet here we have positive proof that the sheer mechanics of fate can take a hand in the life of a man, and decide that he shall live or die!"

123

He went to work again, unbuttoning Allard's shirt, laying it back. Again Doc Sanchez exclaimed, for on Allard's chest, over his heart, was a swelling crimson welt, already beginning to take on the darkness of a savage bruise. Across the hard, sinewy muscles on the other half of his chest was a livid line as though a hot iron had seared the skin without breaking it. And where the right sleeve of the shirt joined at the shoulder was another ragged tear. Doc Sanchez's mild oaths of wonder increased in intensity.

"I'll be damned and double-damned! How close can death breathe on a man and not claim him?"

Doc opened his bag and began smearing the bruise with some kind of pungent ointment, probing gently with his fingers as he worked, while watching Allard's face for some reaction to pain. Not finding what he feared, he nodded with satisfaction.

"No cracked ribs, no deeper hurt than the bruise, though that good heart of yours took a thunderous jolt that would have killed some men. But here the bullet came in at just enough of an angle for the metal of the badge to deflect it. Then it skidded along, barely touching the skin, and went on its way out this hole in your shirt. Man, you figure the percentage of pure chance. I can't."

Now it was Con Waters who came hurrying in, face twisted with honest concern. "Heard the word. Frank Allard—how is he?"

Allard turned his head. "Doing fine, all things concerned. And Shelline...?"

"Dead. You shot him to ribbons. How did it happen?"

Allard explained with brief gravity. Con bobbed his head. "Now it would be like him to sneak back into town, to hide out and try for you from the dark. A crooked tinhorn to the end, dealing from the bottom-of-the-deck."

Doc Sanchez put a medicated compress into place, bandaged it firmly. "Come morning you'll have a mighty sore chest, friend Allard. But there is nothing more I can do for you except give you my blessing."

Allard nodded. "My big thanks, Doc. And Lee, I got a spare shirt somewhere in my junk. Dig it out for me and I'll take up the beat again."

"You will like hell!" snorted Mosby. "You're through for the night. Con and Ben and me, we're shucking the clothes off you and tucking you into bed. Right, Doc?"

"Right!" approved Doc, repacking his bag. "After that savage belt, your heart needs some rest. Don't try to tempt fate, man. You're damned lucky to be alive. If that bullet hadn't struck exactly where it did and from that exact angle, well..." He shrugged.

So that was the way it was, and presently he was alone, with just the low-turned lamp to throw a faint glow across the room. He lay still and marveled at the kiss of fortune. That badge, which he had polished so carefully...!

But for that he'd be lying dead out there in the fevered street, for Shelline's first bullet would have torn through his chest. Fate, so Doc Sanchez had said, had placed that small, thin barrier of metal in front of the lethal lead and deflected it. A miracle—no less! A one in a thousand chance—more, one in ten thousand. The only card in the deck that could have saved him, and it had turned up. What, he wondered, was fate—and where could it lead a man?

The sounds of the street drifted up through his open window. Things were quieting again, though there were still some latecomers out there, arguing over details of the gunplay. But presently these voices drifted away, too. Pawnee, it seemed, was the kind of a town that could take a killing in its stride.

Allard shifted restlessly. What about his part in that affair? He was alive. Harry Shelline was dead. Just like that. A few livid seconds while guns snarled and thudded—and now it was history. It knocked the illusion of life's solidity out of a man. Such a short space of time between living and dying. How could any man be proud?

Ben Ripon came in again, bearing another hot toddy and a small capsule. He dropped the capsule into Allard's hand. "Doc says you're to take this, Mister Allard."

Allard swallowed the capsule, then sipped the toddy. "For a grown man, I've become a damned nuisance, Ben. And you've been mighty good to me."

The little hotelkeeper waved a dismissing hand, showed a faint smile. "A privilege and a pleasure. Got to keep you healthy, as you're good for what ails this damn town." Ripon turned serious. "You think Pinto Jardene set Shelline after you?"

Allard considered for a moment or two. "Could be, Ben. On the other hand, it could have been all Shelline's own idea. You never know what's going on in the mind of a man like Shelline, or what kind of twisted sense of pride they own to."

Ripon nodded. "That's true. Well, the wrong kind of pride has killed men before this. And will again, I suppose."

Drowsiness took hold of Allard. He handed the empty toddy glass back to Ripon and slid down on his pillow, smiling faintly. "Doc Sanchez slipped something over on me in that damned capsule."

He was asleep before Ben Ripon could douse the light and tiptoe out.

Morning's moist freshness poured in through the window and Frank Allard, playing with the idea of getting up and dressing, dropped back on his pillow with a grunt of pained astonishment, his chest was so board stiff it seemed clamped in bands of iron. Ben Ripon, coming in with a tray of food and reading the intent in Allard's expression, wagged a disapproving head.

"You stay put. Doc Sanchez's orders. He'll be up to see you later."

"You'd think I was a damned infant," fumed Allard. "Shelline's bullet never drew even a drop of blood, yet here I am..."

"And there you'll stay!" cut in Ripon. "No, not a drop of blood, true enough. Neither does the kick of a horse draw blood most of the time. But I've yet to hear of a man who absorbed one who didn't notice the aftereffects. So it's another day in bed for you, my friend."

"We'll see," growled Allard. "I'll argue that point with Doc."

Steaming coffee and warm breakfast and a cigar to top it off improved matters considerably, and Allard was fairly cheerful when Doc Sanchez, an hour later, came in at his bustling walk. As Doc began peeling the compress off Allard's chest, Allard said, "Ben Ripon gave me some kind of cock-and-bull story of me having to stay in bed today, Doc."

"You'll stay," affirmed Doc tartly, unless you've got no sense at all. We'll admit you got a heart like a horse. If you didn't have, the shock of that blow could have killed you just as dead as if the bullet had gone straight through. A bruise like this reaches deep and unless handled right, can kick up all kinds of complications. In the interest of medical science, if not your own well-being, you'll do it."

Allard nodded, drawling. "Just as you say, Doc—just as you say. You're convincing, if nothing else."

Doc's lips twitched slightly. "Seen some bruises in my time, but nothing to beat this one. Have a look."

Allard twisted his head and looked down. All the left side of his chest was discolored. He flinched as Doc smeared on some kind of salve and began kneading the area with deft, gentle fingers. "Where," asked Doc, "did you learn to shoot like that? You hit Shelline three times, and any one of them was a fatal wound."

"I don't recall doing anything because of deliberate thought," Allard answered with slow soberness. "It was all just instinct, I guess."

"Damned efficient instinct, I'd say," observed Doc dryly. "Now hang onto yourself. I'm going to dig a little deeper, and it'll hurt."

It did hurt, plenty. Allard squirmed and swore, but presently, as Doc's ministrations began to loosen up the stiffened muscles, the effect became almost soothing. Doc grinned, "Better, eh?"

"A lot," Allard agreed, sweating a little. "Just the same, I think I will stick close to this bed for a while, after all."

"If you don't," Doc threatened, "I'll slug you with another capsule."

Smeared with ointment, bandaged, and reasonably comfortable, Allard set himself to patiently wait the day's hours through. A locomotive whistle bayed in distant loneliness, and shortly after this, Allard picked up another sound, still faint with distance, the ragged bellowing of cattle on the move. Another trail herd was moving in toward the shipping pens, coming up out of the wide, empty country to the south.

Sometime later, Lee Mosby came in, bringing with him Allard's gun and another badge. The gun was freshly cleaned and oiled and loaded. Allard took the weapon with thanks and pushed it under his pillow. But he shook his head at the badge.

"I'm going to keep on wearing the old one, Lee— battered and bent, just as it is. I figure it good luck. Man, you look tired."

"Fairly busy night," Mosby admitted. "Town simmered for quite awhile over the shooting. Then there were a couple of other things."

"What other things?"

Mosby shrugged. "Like this. Hear that herd coming in? Well, around midnight, making the rounds, I dropped into the Palace. Abel Starke and some of his Slash S outfit were there, along with another rider who had just come into town from the south. This one is named Brack Harper, so I heard him called. From the talk going on, I gathered that he's the owner of this new herd, and he was wild-eyed about a rustling raid pulled on his herd back along the trail a ways. Him and Starke had their heads together, and all the signs point to their cooking up some kind of trouble over their stolen cattle. It was around three o'clock this morning before things quieted down enough for me to take a chance on getting some sleep."

Allard studied the big, fair-haired man standing beside his bed. It might have been imagination, but it seemed to him that Lee Mosby's face had grown less heavy, that a firm, muscled leanness was taking over. It was as though the reawakening of pride and purpose in the man had caused him to shed the soft tissue of mental and physical apathy. His eyes were tired, but they held a spark.

Seeming to understand the thought that lay behind Allard's appraisal, Mosby colored slightly and spoke with some gruffness. "Yeah, I'm up off my belly, Frank. And I like the change so well I aim to stay this way. There's some who hate me for it, but by God, they don't look down their noses at me anymore!"

"Earning the hate of the wrong kind, Lee, is just as big a tribute to a man as earning the liking and respect of the right kind," Allard told him. "About Starke and that other fellow getting together to cook up possible trouble, I doubt anything will break until this new herd is loaded and all hands free to start their hell raising. By that time I'll be up and with you again."

Mosby nodded. "You're probably right, there. But about these rustling deals, Frank—what's a man to think? These two raids were pretty heavy ones, apparently—the kind no herd owner can or is willing to stand for and is about to shrug off. An angle that has me fighting my head is this. Where around here would a couple of fairly large jags of rustled cattle be driven to? Where would they be held? Also, how would they be disposed of? Men don't run the risks of a rustling raid, just for the hell of it. I tell you I've been banging my head against the wall, trying to dredge up an answer that would make sense. So far I haven't had a bit of luck."

"Get me right. I'm not in favor of that sort of business any time, any place," Allard said. "But, after all, this affair is really no concern of ours. We keep the lid on here in town, which is about all we can do. Anything that takes place outside of town is somebody else's worry, not ours. Seen anything of Pinto Jardene since last night's trouble?"

"No. But I did pass Haley Twitchell just leaving the Palace. He looked pretty sour, as though he was upset over something."

Allard's faint smile held little of mirth. "Disappointed, no doubt, that Shelline didn't have any better luck."

Mosby swung his head. "You really think Haley Twitchell has it in for you that bad, Frank?"

"Him and that lovely son of his, both. They play close to Jardene, don't they? Well, all the same basket of snakes. And, Lee—don't you go getting careless, now that they don't like you anymore. They might try cooking up the same sort of thing for you that they did for me. You watch the dark corners. Kind of surprises me that Pinto Jardene hasn't called you in and tried to give you your walking papers."

Mosby grinned down at Allard. "Probably because he realizes he wouldn't have any more luck with me that way than he did with you. Man, did you ever stop to consider what damn foolishness it is for you and me to go on risking our skins for a town that's rapidly getting no use for either of us?"

"Not all the town," Allard corrected. "Lot of good people in Pawnee. And when you think of everything, it's kind of a satisfying damn foolishness, don't you think, Lee?"

Moving to the door, Mosby paused and considered

for a moment. Then he nodded. "Yes, it is. But damned if I ever thought I'd feel that way about it. Well, take it easy."

The day ran along and Allard slept for a time while noon came and passed. When he awoke, all was clamor reaching up from the loading pens. The usual jumble of noise. Bawl of harried, weary cattle, the shrill voices of trail hands, the snorting and bell-clanging of the locomotive spotting cars.

A feeling of physical wholeness had returned to Frank Allard. Doc Sanchez's wise ministrations had taken effect. His chest was still tender and sore, but that stifling stricture of stiffness was pretty well gone. He'd be up and on duty again this night.

Came a soft step in the hall and a small, almost hesitant knock. Then it was Nell Kane who slipped into the room. She was breathing fast as though she had been running. She came to the edge of the bed and looked down at Frank Allard, her eyes wide and dark.

"I—I had to come and see with my own eyes that you were all right. Con Waters said that you were. But Sam and I—we wanted to be sure."

Sam and I! Allard pondered these words as he stared up at her.

"Yes, Nell, I'm doing fine. Be up and around again this evening. Child, it was nice of you to come and see me."

She was a girl with a strong grace in her as she stood limned against afternoon's light flooding in at the window. She spoke again, her words quick.

"I wanted to thank you, too, for being friendly with Sam and for advising him. We'll both remember you kindly for that, always."

Allard pushed up on his right elbow. "Nell, you talk like you and Sam Lorry had ideas. Like you might be considering leaving these parts. Is that so?"

She nodded with a quick eagerness, pressing her hands together in a small gesture of nervousness. "Yes,

Sam wants me to go with him—and I want to go. I'm going to go! Sam and I, we knew how we felt about each other from the very first. And last night, after that shooting affair, Mister Paxton was out of the store for a time, and Sam and I, we had a chance to talk things over. We'll go south. Coming up the drive trail, Sam saw a lot of country down there, good country, where young folks can make a start. We'll be married there. Sam says he'll work hard and so will I. We'll make out."

Allard was still for a moment while he thought. "What will Gil Paxton have to say about it?"

She tossed her head with a hint of the old rebellious defiance. "What can he say after we're gone? Oh, I'd like to have him feel kindly toward us, for in his way I guess he's been good to me. But when I've tried to talk to him about such things he gets very angry and won't listen. I've tried and tried to make him understand, like Jim Creightly understood and like I know you do. But he won't."

"When do you and Sam figure on leaving, Nell?"

"At the first good chance. As soon as Sam can locate a horse for me and get together the gear he needs. Do—do you think we're doing right?"

He studied her gravely. Here was no sullen, caged girl, desperate for life, full of starved and thwarted emotions that were ready to explode and drive her down any dark trail, just so it led to some semblance of the freedom she craved. Instead, it seemed he could glimpse a sort of inner glow in her, a certain full sweetness of spirit that had come to her on the wings of the romance for which she'd hungered so. And yet, still a slightly uncertain youngster wanting the approval of an older head on the step she was about to take. Allard's tone ran gentle.

"Yes, Nell, you're right, both of you. You have every right to live your own life. And Sam Lorry is a good, sound, square man. I wish you both all the best of luck and I know you'll be happy. Don't worry too much about Gil Paxton. Give him time and he'll get over it."

"I—I'm not too sure of that," she said hesitantly. "Sometimes I think there is a side to him that nobody sees. When he is very angry, he turns strange in a way that frightens me. And I better go now, before he finds out that I'm not home. And thanks so much for understanding."

Allard pushed a little higher, the shadow of a grimness gathered in his eyes. "I'd like to ask you a couple of questions before you leave, Nell. The night Jim Creightly was killed—where were you?"

Startled, she stared at him. "Why, I was tending store. Mister Paxton had gone out on an errand of some sort."

"As you remember it, Nell, what happened?"

The girl picked her words carefully. "I was alone in the store, tidying up some goods on the shelves. There was a shot out in the street and then some excitement. Right after that, Mr. Paxton and Con Waters came in, carrying Jim Creightly between them. Mr. Paxton was very upset. He sent me upstairs. Sometime later he came up and told me Jim Creightly was dead. It was a terrible night. For I liked Jim Creightly. He was good and kind to me—and he understood."

Allard let himself back slowly to the pillow. "Thanks, Nell—thanks a lot. Now you better scatter along. It was mighty fine of you to come and see me. I'll look up Sam Lorry tomorrow. I'll help him get that horse for you, and see that he has an outfit for the trail."

Her eyes were luminous as she looked down at him. Then, in swift impulsiveness she bent and brushed her 'ips against his cheek. "I knew you'd understand," she murmured.

At the door someone cleared his throat. It was Lafe Oglevie and just past his shoulder it was Barbara Chancellor who stood there. Nell Kane, with a small gasp of consternation, straightened up. Allard, startled himself, exclaimed. "More visitors! This is fine—fine! Come in, folks—come in!"

The moment the doorway was clear, Nell Kane whisked through it and was gone. Lafe Oglevie, coming up beside the bed, rumbled, "Now I hope Barbara and me didn't butt in where we weren't wanted?"

"Far from it," drawled Allard quietly. "Kind of you to drop by." He looked at Barbara Chancellor. "Won't you take the chair?"

"Thanks," she answered stiffly. "We're not staying long."

She moved to the window and stared out of it. Her lips were compressed and her back very straight. There fell a short silence, which Lafe Oglevie hurried to fill.

"Word reached the ranch about your affair with Shelline. From the account we got, you were in bed, but nobody seemed to know for sure just how bad you were hurt. So Barbara and me, we decided to ride in and find out firsthand. You seem pretty chipper."

"Little wrong with me," declared Allard. "But you can't argue with Doc Sanchez when he gets his neck bowed. I'll be up and on duty again this evening."

"Just what happened, anyhow?" asked Lafe.

Allard gave him the story briefly. "More luck than sense," he concluded. "One good thing came out of the affair, though. It showed me how many good friends I'd made in a short time."

Barbara Chancellor turned and looked at him, a strange storminess in her eyes. Her voice was brittle. "Very good friends indeed—some of them—it would seem."

Lafe Oglevie cleared his throat again, began fumbling in his pockets for a smoke. Allard met Barbara's glance steadily. He smiled. "I'm sure of that."

Barbara marched to the door. "I'll wait for you downstairs, Lafe. It seems there was no great cause for our anxiety over Mister Allard."

Allard's smile persisted. "At least it was anxiety. You got no idea how much that means to me."

Barbara's glance was withering. "I can imagine! I'm glad to know you were being comforted so capably."

She was gone, the tapping of her heels a fading but crisp staccato.

Lafe Oglevie sighed heavily. "Why in hell didn't you have a warning sign hung on your door? Barbara was all set to make you happy by bringing you a touch of woman's sympathy. And then we walk in on something like that."

Allard's tone sharpened a trifle. "Like what, Lafe?"

"Well," floundered Lafe, "That Kane girl was kissing you, wasn't she? Me, I don't embarrass easy, but about then I was all thumbs and left feet. You can imagine how Barbara felt."

"Lafe," said Allard evenly, "you're a good guy and I like you. But right now you're being thick-headed as a lost burro. There are things going on that you don't know anything about, but none of them are cause for you to hide your head in shame—or me, either. I'd like to hear you apologize to Nell Kane."

Lafe Oglevie stared at him, then the big foreman's leonine grin showed. "All right, I apologize. But I bet Barbara is fit to start bustin' crockery about now."

"Why the devil should she?" demanded Allard. "What possible concern could she have in me, or whether Nell Kane does or doesn't kiss me?"

Lafe shrugged his big shoulders. "Women—just the makeup of the critters. That answers plenty of questions. Then again, there never has been any love lost between Barbara Chancellor and Nell Kane. Two pretty girls squaring off at each other, you know. And Nell Kane always has believed that John Chancellor lynched her father."

"Well, didn't he?"

"Hell, no! Shark Knoles did."

"Who's Shark Knoles?"

135

"A Bench cattleman. Ornery old blister. Runs a two-bit spread way back against the Vestals. Oh, there was no question about Luke Kane being a cow thief, and I guess he had a rope coming. But John Chancellor and the C Cross had no hand in it. This affair of yours with Shelline—you figure Pinto Jardene may have sent him against you?"

"Could be, but hard to say for sure. Anyhow, I was lucky."

"That you were," declared Oglevie fervently. "Well, now that I know you're able to sit up and take nourishment, I'll be on my way. And you keep a better eye on dark corners after this."

CHAPTER NINE

FRANK ALLARD walked along a street shrouded in the hush of twilight. He felt pretty much his usual self, aside from a lingering soreness and stiffness across his chest muscles. He had sent Ben Ripon after Doc Sanchez, and then stated his flat determination to get up and around again in time to take over his duties for the night. Doc had cussed him a little before giving in. And now it was good to be free of the confines of his bed.

He turned in at Con Waters' livery barn, went back through the dark gloom of the place to where his roan was stalled, and with a curry comb he'd taken from a rack by the main door, began working on the animal. A moment later Con's voice reached him.

"Of all the darn fools! And you just out of a sick bed. That bronc has already been worked on. Stable fee for a bronc takes in a good currying and brushin' down once a day."

Allard turned as Con came hurrying up. "I know Con. But I kind of like to fuss with this old knothead. Been over considerable trail together, the roan and me. Besides, it's good to have an honest bronc to turn to when you get fed up with humans."

"Now," said Con, "I know what you mean." He was silent for a moment before adding soberly, "Frank, what are we going to do about Nell Kane and that young Slash S rider, Sam Lorry?"

Allard came fully around. "Meaning what, Con?"

Con bobbed his head. "You know. You're not blind, nor am I. Sam Lorry's been trying to trade me out of a horse. He's already got one horse. So what would a lad like him be wantin' a second one for if it wasn't for somebody else to ride?"

Allard came out of the stall, knocking the curry comb against a partition to clean it. "Con," he murmured, "you're a wise old mick. So you and me better have a talk, right here and now."

They hunkered down on soft straw, their backs against an oat bin. "What's your feeling in the matter, Con?" Allard asked.

"Why," said Con, "I'm tryin' to remember that there's a fine shine to the world when you're young. Your dreams are big and they reach to hell an' gone, and there ain't anything life can throw at you that you're afraid of. You can take on life without a thin dime in your pocket, and laugh at it. Takes age to soften up a man and make him cautious and afraid. Well, Nell and Sam got little more than that thin dime, outside of youth and its courage and great dreams. But who's got the right to deny them their try at life?"

"Exactly!" Allard twisted up a cigarette. "So you're going to let Sam have that horse?"

"I'm weakening," Con admitted. "But I'm also thinking and worrying some about Gil Paxton and what he

138

will have to say. If I could figger an answer to Gil, why then the rest would be easy. I might even slip a couple of hundred into Nell's hand to smooth the trail a mite. For I'm fond of Nell. And Sam's a good, steady likable sort."

Allard dropped a hand on one of Con's gaunt knees, gave it a squeeze. "My sentiments all the way, Con. Why worry about Paxton? He'll just have to make the best of it."

Con built a little mound of straw in front of him, then knocked it aside with a quick brush of his hand. "I've known Gil Paxton a long time. Him and me, we're two of the real old-timers in this town. Lot of things about Gil I like a heap. But..."

"But what, Con?" urged Allard intently.

"Well, there's an angle to Gil Paxton I don't know at all," Con admitted slowly. "That nobody knows, I guess. A few times I've glimpsed it, and when I did, saw a strange darkness there. Lookin' back, I think the first time I noticed that darkness it was after his wife left him."

"Heard about that," Allard put in.

"Aye," nodded Con. "And a fine, spirited woman she was, too. But in the monotony of running that store the sweetness drained out of her and a sort of sullen rebellion took its place. Couple of times I tried to talk to Gil about it, suggesting that he close up for a spell or get somebody to run his store for a month or two while he took his wife away for a change of scenery—someplace where she could pretty up and taste some of the things in life a woman hungers for. Pretty clothes—a little gaiety. I didn't get no place. Gil told me to mind my business. So I did—and then it happened. The first train going out of this town, she went on it. Some say with a man from the survey gang. I wouldn't know for sure. All I am sure of is that I like to remember Mrs. Paxton as a fine lady."

A short silence fell. Then Allard spoke softly. "That could explain why Paxton feels as he does about Nell."

Con Waters bobbed his head again. "I think so. Gil's fond of Nell, that I know. But it is not a generous fondness. With Gil it is a possessive thing, and it rises from something inside the man that's part of that strange darkness I see. Mebbe that sounds kinda mixed up, but it's the best I can do. Words never did come easy to me."

"I'd say you've made it clear enough, Con," said Allard gravely. "Better yet, I think you and me understand each other pretty well. So I'm going to lay some cards on the table. I'm going to ask you some straight questions and I want some straight answers. It has to do with Jim Creightly's death. Shall I go on, Con?"

Con Waters was very still. Then he let out a deep, slow sigh. "Now I knew that would come, sooner or later, for I've recognized a shrewdness in you from the very first. Yes, it was bound to come. Go on, man."

"I've had Gil Paxton's version of Jim Creightly's death," Allard said. "Part of the story as Paxton told it was true, but a lot of it wasn't. Why wasn't it? Paxton said that after the shot was fired, somebody ran down the street. But nobody ran down the street, Con."

The stable owner racked his shoulders back against the oat bin, and his tone was bleak with misery.

"When a man is your longtime friend, and when you know there is much good in him, why, then you try and give him the benefit of the doubt. I've tried to give Gil Paxton that benefit, but there's a black devil that's lived and lived with me...." Con's words frittered out and his gaunt shoulders slumped again. Allard waited, and presently Con's head came up once more.

"No, Frank Allard, there was nobody runnin' down the street. I'd have heard it if Gil did, for I was out in the street before the echoes of the shot had died. And Gil didn't come out of the store."

"Of course he didn't," agreed Allard. "Because he

wasn't in the store when the shot was fired. Nell Kane was in there alone. And if Paxton wasn't in the store, where was he, Con? And why should he claim that he was?"

Con pushed to his feet, his hands spread helplessly. "Don't ask me anymore, for I don't know. I can't even think of a single man in this town that Gil Paxton would be covering up for. Yet it must be so. Ah, it was a fine evenin' until you came in here to ask questions of me...."

There was no falsity in Con Waters. This was a sincere man. Allard, also on his feet now, put a hand on Con's shoulder.

"We'll forget about that angle now, Con. We'll think of better things. About a young pair of folks and their future. Sam Lorry gets that horse, Con—and you see to it that it is a good one. I'll stand the cost. And there is something else. From a remark or two I happened to hear, I understand there's a piece of range on the Bench that belonged to Nell's father, and now to her. What do you know about that?"

"There is such a bit of land," Con said. "Not a great deal. A quarter section, about. But with fine water, and reasonably valuable because of that. Why do you ask?"

"Because, when they leave, Nell Kane and Sam Lorry will be heading for a new country, away from old memories that might plague Nell. They won't be back. And why should Nell leave a piece of range and lose it all, when by selling it she could have a little stake for her and Sam to work on? At a guess, what would you say the place is worth?"

Con pursed his lips, considered thoughtfully. "As things go in this country, say twenty-five hundred dollars. But who would stand ready to buy it right now, even if they could?"

"I would, for one," Allard told him.

"You!" Con stared. "And what would you want with it?"

While talking, they had moved slowly out of the stable, and now stood in the darkening street. Allard looked past the corner of the stable toward the lift of the wide reaches of the Bench, eyes narrowed, features set in sober reflection.

"I've no roots set anywhere just now, Con. And if I don't set them pretty quick, maybe I never will. There's a look to the Bench country that I like. Why shouldn't I start digging in there?"

"But you'd have to get an answer from Gil Paxton on such a deal," warned Con. "He's Nell's guardian."

"Assumed, maybe. But not necessarily legally. In any case I intend to look into the matter. And now, Con, just you and me and these stable walls have heard this talk. I'd like it to stay that way."

"That's the way it will be," promised Con.

Allard went off down the deep dusk of the street, heading for the office. Lights were beginning to glimmer through town, but the office was still dark. Allard went in, found a chair, and settled back with his thoughts. Half an hour later, Lee Mosby came in.

"Town's quiet, Lee," murmured Allard.

"Too damn quiet," Mosby growled. "Ain't natural this way with a couple of trail crews on the loose. Just took a look in at the Palace as I came by. Abel Starke and Brack Harper are in there again, their heads together. I tell you those fellows are cooking up something. Sure you ought to be up and around this way?"

"Quite sure. I feel fine. And I'll handle things all right tonight."

"Then I'll turn in early," Mosby yawned. "But I'll sleep light, and in case you need me I won't be far away. And you watch those dark corners, fellah. Because you've used up your share of luck."

Mosby went into the rear room, and a bunk creaked as he settled down on it. His boots thumped hollowly on the floor as he pulled them off and dropped them.

"Herding humans into line can sure get damned

monotonous," he called, grumbling. "Never realized how much until lately."

Allard smiled through the darkness. "For a steady chore, Lee—I'll still take cattle. Well, I'm on my way."

His first stop was at the Palace. He went in quietly, had his look around. Men watched him covertly, noting the dented, twisted badge on his shirt, a badge marked with the gray streaks of crushed lead, and their expressions showed mingled awe and respect. For here was a man who had shaken hands with death and then walked away.

Surveying the place, Allard saw no sign of Pinto Jardene and, struck with a sudden hard decision of purpose which carved his mouth into harshness, walked back to the door of the rear room. A bouncer, sitting in a chair beside the door, got to his feet, barring Allard's way.

"Pinto's busy."

"Not that busy," shot back Allard. "Get out of my way!"

The last words had a low, curt ring to them, and there was level ice in Allard's eyes. The bouncer was a hulking fellow and was not afraid to move into a barroom brawl any time such a problem arose. But this was different. His pouched, booze-reddened eyes touched that battered badge on Allard's shirt, flickered up to meet Allard's glance, then flickered away again. Here was the man who had downed Harry Shelline, after Shelline had had first bite. The bouncer was superstitious. He stepped aside.

Allard pushed the door open and went through. At that poker table in the room's center, with its overhead cone of light, sat Pinto Jardene. He had two companions. One of these was Abel Starke. The other was a stranger to Allard, a well set-up man of middle age, with a long, hard jaw and deep-set eyes. There were neither poker chips or cards in front of them.

Pinto Jardene's eyes took on that hard, black shine

and he pushed his chair back from the table. "Allard, I told you once—!"

"Tonight I'm telling you," cut in Allard. "Get this, Jardene—get it good—get all of it! I don't know whether you set Shelline after me or whether it was all his own idea. Neither do I expect you to put me right about it, for the truth would probably choke in your throat. But this I do know. Another try of the same sort by one of your crowd, and I'll be certain it's your doings. So then—I come after you—and I come all the way! That clear?"

Pinto Jardene sat there, saying nothing, but hating—hating darkly, poisonously. Those black eyes seemed to glaze over. But still he said nothing. Allard's glance touched Abel Starke.

"For an honest cattleman, Starke, you're in damn poor company."

He moved to the door then, watching them. Then he swung it open and stepped through. He went along the bar, pausing only long enough to buy a couple of cigars, then moved out into the street. Just beyond the fanning light from the Palace door he stopped to get one of the cigars alight. A voice reached him from the shadows, a voice he recognized instantly. The voice of Haley Twitchell.

"I'd like a few words with you, Allard—if you can spare the time."

For a long moment or two, Allard studied the dark, his hand stealing toward his gun. After the Shelline experience he'd be a fool to take anything for granted. Haley Twitchell seemed to read Allard's thoughts, for he quickly added, "There's no danger in me, man. This talk will be all to your advantage."

Allard moved over that way, relaxing a little. "All right," he said crisply. "I'm willing to listen." He could make out the banker's stocky figure now.

"Be more comfortable in my office," said Twitchell. Wondering about this, Allard followed along.

Twitchell unlocked a side door of the bank, and after lighting a lamp in his office, the banker turned it down to a faint glow. From a deep desk drawer he brought out a bottle and two glasses, poured short drinks.

"Good stuff," he said, pushing one of the glasses across to Allard. "Bonded. Not bar poison. Looking at you!"

It was good bourbon all right, smooth and mellow. Twitchell freshened the glasses, leaned back.

"You're curious, of course. Well, this won't take long. As a banker, Allard, it's my business to face facts. So I never dodge them, nor have I any use for sentiment in business. Putting it bluntly, in you I see a tough man—and, I believe, a practical one. Frankly, I'd feel a lot more comfortable if you were a long ways from Pawnee instead of sitting right here in front of me. Don't ask me why I feel that way, but I have my reasons. Now then, for something I want, I'm always willing to pay. What is it worth to you to roll your pack tonight, saddle your horse, and head out of Pawnee and this part of the country for good?"

The inscrutable mask settled over Allard's face. He pulled on his cigar while twirling the liquor glass between his fingers on the smooth desk top. His thoughts were far within him. When he finally answered, it was slowly. "What would it be worth to you to have me gone?"

Twitchell opened another drawer of the desk and came up with a well-padded envelope. "There's a thousand dollars here, Allard. All yours if you'll be long gone by daylight tomorrow. A thousand dollars. Take you a long time to earn that much on the pay you draw as night marshal. Well, there it is. What do you say?"

Why? The question was scrambling through Allard's mind from all odd directions, seeking an answer that made logic and sense. A thousand dollars was money, a lot of money—even to a banker. What possible effect could his presence have on any of Haley Twitchell's affairs that Twitchell valued a thousand dollars worth? It couldn't be personal fear. Unless....

Allard's shadowed eyes took in the banker, took in all of him and wondered if a man like this had shot Jim Creightly in the back; wondered if in some way Twitchell had got an inkling as to the real purpose behind Allard's presence in Pawnee, and was trying to buy his way out? Or perhaps Twitchell was the man Gil Paxton was trying to cover up for. Perhaps Paxton owed Twitchell money and for that reason was willing to cover Twitchell's hide.

No, that couldn't be it. Neither of these surmises came up real. Somehow, as he considered things, Allard knew that these were not the answer. He took another slow pull at his cigar.

"I don't get it, Twitchell. What have you to fear from me? You run your bank, you play a little poker. We'll say that you just don't like me. But there's nothing there that shapes up as breaking any law. So I just can't see where I'm of enough concern to you in any way that would warrant you paying me a thousand dollars to jump the country. Where's the joker in this pack?"

"If there is one, like I said before, it's no concern of yours," answered the banker heavily. "I've my own reasons and they're good enough for me. Know of any way you can earn a thousand dollars more easily? Just take the money, saddle up and drift. You drifted into Pawnee. You drift out, a thousand dollars to the good. Simple as that. Well...?"

Allard picked up the envelope, balanced it in his fingers, his glance boring at the banker. A gross man in several ways, this Haley Twitchell, with his heavy lips sagging slightly and stained around the edges with the juice of countless chewed cigars.

Allard showed a small, mirthless smile. "A man does bump into the damndest things! Anybody would think

I breathed fire and brimstone. What are you afraid of, Twitchell?"

The banker flushed. "Being afraid or not afraid doesn't enter at all. I've given it to you straight from the shoulder. For my own reasons. And I've made it well worth your while."

"Worth my while!" murmured Allard. "I wonder. I wonder if a man's self-respect isn't worth considerably more than a thousand dollars?"

Haley Twitchell's neck seemed to swell a little. "I'll make it fifteen hundred. But that's positively my last offer."

Allard dropped the envelope back on the desk, and his tone went curtly harsh. "Bribe declined! I aim to stick around awhile, if for no other reason than to find out why it was offered. You know, Twitchell, fellows like you who deal only in money, so often make the same mistake. You figure that money can buy anything. So many times it can. But this isn't one of them!"

Allard got up and moved toward the door. The banker spoke again, and quickly. "Fifteen hundred dollars, Allard. A lot of money."

"Save your damned money," retorted Allard curtly. "I wouldn't touch it if it were a million!"

The Bench lay verdant under the sun's midday warmth. Almost prairielike in its broad, slightly rolling miles was this great tableland. Blue-black against the far northern reaches, the timber clad Vestals combed the sky. Patches of that timber, like flecks of substance thrown off by some parent body, made scattered islands of shadow against the long, smooth run of the thick-grassed earth. Closer to the Vestals, the timber spilled down and ran out in reaching fingers that finally thinned and dwindled to a stop.

The trail swept on in broad curves and straight running tangents, threading a way past the timber islands. Along it, Frank Allard's roan kept to a steady jog. Riding loose and easy in the saddle, Allard reveled in the empty, almost drowsy peace of this Bench country, but did this with a sort of secondary consciousness, for the core of his mind was working somberly with a number of nagging, questioning thoughts.

He had carried these thoughts with him and argued with them through all of last night's solitary, almost ominously peaceful patrol of Pawnee's dives and deadfalls; thoughts that had kept him from finding immediate sleep when he turned in finally in the cold, early hours of the morning, and thoughts that had been there to greet him when he awoke only an hour or so ago. Thoughts always preceded by one nagging word; why?

First, why had Gil Paxton given him an untrue picture concerning the killing of Jim Creightly?

Again, why would Abel Starke, owner of the Slash S herd, and Brack Harper, owner of the latest trail herd to be shipped, for so had Allard been able to identify the man, have been sitting in close conference with Pinto Jardene in the latter's private back room in the Palace, when only a day or two previous Abel Starke was ready to approve his riders' tearing the Palace apart?

And why should Haley Twitchell offer him, Frank Allard, as much as fifteen hundred dollars if he'd drift the country? Finally, aside from their individual significance, was there any chance that all these things were tied together in some larger meaning?

Why—why—why—?

Allard struck the flat of his hand against his saddle horn. Questions—questions—questions. And no good answer to any of them. The only thing he could be sure of was that Lee Mosby had in no way exaggerated things when he said that Pawnee was full of shady crosscurrents and politics, and that no matter which way a man with a badge moved, he'd find himself crowding somebody.

Allard pushed all this confusion of mental clutter aside and gave himself over to the sheer luxury of being alone in open, fair country, with the sense of freedom and relaxation it gave to a man. He drank in the wide distances, savored the good flavor of the sun and the breath of the earth, and let run out of him all the tensions that Pawnee and its problems had saddled upon him.

He began seeing cattle, some grazing, some resting in the shade of the timber islands. On most of these he read the Chancellor Iron, the C Cross, though here and there he picked up an odd brand like the Box K, the J S Connected, and the Triple X. White-faced cattle mostly, with some off-strains showing. But cattle, fat cattle, on fat range, the way the Lord intended cattle to be, and the Lord's good privilege for a man to ride among them. Frank Allard's distaste for his role in Pawnee deepened.

The trail dipped straight into the middle of one of the larger timber islands, and here the air lay still and cool and rich with the piny fragrance of conifers, and here also stood two ground-reined saddle mounts and on a small log beside the trail sat Barbara Chancellor and Royce Twitchell.

Hiding his small start of surprise, Allard touched his hat and spoke his quick apology. "Sorry if I'm trespassing. Didn't mean to." He looked directly at the girl.

He couldn't be sure, but it struck him that there was a faint flush of some kind of emotion in Barbara's face and, at this moment also, a spark of relief in her eyes. But her answer was tautly curt.

"The trail's free."

"Thanks," murmured Allard. "And I take it this one leads to the C Cross headquarters?"

"It does. You've business there?"

Allard nodded. "Of a sort. Wanted a talk with Lafe Oglevie."

His glance touched Royce Twitchell and saw no friendliness there at all. Instead he saw only a slow fuming anger in young Twitchell's eyes, together with pointed dislike, and both reflected in Twitchell's tone. "Out-of-bounds, aren't you, Allard? Your job's in town."

Allard shrugged. "Night's when I work. Rest of the time's my own." He looked at the girl again. "Thanks for the directions."

He lifted the reins and the roan moved on. There was a stir of movement behind him, the creak of saddle leather, a low-toned word or two, and then, as he rode out of the timber into the sunlit open again, Barbara Chancellor came up beside him.

"I'm heading home. I'll show you the way." There was something like defiance in her manner and tone.

Knowing a small shade of inner amusement, Allard tipped his head. "Privilege on my part. But will it meet with Royce Twitchell's approval?"

Now she did color, furiously. "What I do is subject to nobody's approval but my own."

Allard smiled faintly. "Fine thing, independence."

They rode along in a silence that Barbara finally broke. "I wonder that you are able to tear yourself away from town, what with all your—your friends there."

"Fine thing, friends," observed Allard evenly. "Figured I might have a couple of such up here on the Bench. Like Lafe Oglevie—and you."

"Perhaps acquaintance would be the better word," she retorted tartly.

Open amusement etched wrinkles at the corners of Allard's eyes. "Real scratchy today, aren't you? And you shouldn't be. Too fine a day for that. The kind of day that does things to you—good things. Builds deep lights in your hair, puts a glow in your cheeks. Friend of yours, this sun is. Makes you lovely."

She came around in her saddle at this, her eyes wide and startled, then going for a brief moment almost girlishly soft and shy. But as swiftly as it came, this expression left, and her stiff reticence returned.

"We'll not discuss me, if you please. What do you want to see Lafe Oglevie about?"

"Things," said Allard quietly.

"What kind of things?"

"Man talk."

She seemed to feel that this shut her out completely, and from then on she said no word, just rode with her shoulders erect and her eyes straight ahead. The trail unwound ever deeper toward the Vestals until, when they cut past the tip of a down-reaching finger of timber, the C Cross headquarters came into view.

A big, solid-looking spread, taking in all of the upper end of an extensive meadow. As Allard and Barbara Chancellor rode up, it was Lafe Oglevie who came up to a corral fence, beyond which a couple of the C Cross crew had a hand forge going and were sweating over the job of shoeing several cavvy broncs.

Lafe climbed the fence and took the rein of Barbara's horse as she swung down and headed for the low, spreading log-built ranch house without a word or backward look.

The foreman looked at Allard with raised eyebrows. "She rode out a couple of hours ago with young Royce Twitchell, now she rides back with you. Where was the switch made?"

"Back along the trail a piece," explained Allard. "Sort of stumbled into her, and she showed me the way here. Doesn't seem to like me, though."

"With reason?"

Allard's tone sharpened a little. "Be your age, man. Anybody else but you make that crack, I'd take a swing at them."

"Forget it," said Oglevie, beginning to loosen the latigo of the girl's saddle. "It's only that I feel a lot of responsibility for Barbara. Before he died, John Chancellor asked me to do my best by Barbara. I aim to. What brings you out here—just the idea of a ride?"

"Part that, part something else. How far from here are the old Kane holdings?"

Lafe Oglevie came around, looked up at Allard. "Fair jaunt. What's your interest there?"

"Why," said Allard slowly, "I might buy the place if it suits me."

Oglevie studied him intently for a moment, then turned back and finished the chore of unsaddling Barbara's mount and turning it into a corral. His leonine brow was furrowed with thought as he came slowly over to Allard again.

"You know that Barbara would like to buy that place herself?"

Allard nodded. "Heard her mention something to that effect that day you and I met her on the trail, heading for town. But she hasn't had any luck there, has she? Well, I figured I might. Anything wrong in that?"

"No-o," said Oglevie slowly. He scrubbed his chin with thumb and forefinger. "You'll have better luck finding the place if I ride with you. Wait till I catch and saddle."

Five minutes later they were on their way, heading a little southwest. "Joins up with the C Cross range on the west," explained Lafe Oglevie. "Plume Creek flows through it. Any of my business why you want to own it?"

"Hell, no—not at all," answered Allard easily. "Comes a day in a man's life when he realizes it's high time to set his roots permanent. That day has arrived with me. I heard of the place and I like this country. So..." He shrugged.

"What makes you think you'll have better luck talking business to that Kane girl than Barbara had? And what will Gil Paxton have to say about it?"

"Lot of maybes there," admitted Allard. "But I'll never find out until I try. Right now I want to see if the place is worth the effort."

"Night marshal must pay pretty good money," said Oglevie slyly.

Allard reared back in his saddle. "Lafe, you're working up to an argument. What the devil did you mean by that crack?"

"Trying to get some answers," said Oglevie coolly. "Some things for you to remember. Man to man I got to admit I like you. But over and above everything else, I'm C Cross, all the way, come hell, fire, or blue thunder."

"Good!" snapped Allard. "You be all of that, and more credit to you. But don't also be a thick-headed damn fool. I'm playing this thing square. You ought to know that. Would I have come to you if I wasn't?"

Oglevie considered this for a moment, then nodded. "That's right," he admitted gruffly. "Sorry. But I've the feeling of something queer going on in these parts, so I'm not taking anything for granted. Yeah, I got that uneasy feeling up and down my back, but damned if I can put my finger on the cause of it."

Allard's annoyance ran out of him. "There are queer things in the wind, Lafe. Things like these." He went on to tell of seeing Abel Starke and Brack Harper in conference of some sort with Pinto Jardene. And then of Haley Twitchell's amazing offer if he'd skip the country. "See if you can find an answer to those two things. Damned if I can, and I've been pulling my brains apart ever since."

Lafe Oglevie swore with soft wonder. "There might be a dozen reasons why them two cattlemen were having a talk with Jardene. But Twitchell's attempt to buy you off whips me. I've known Haley Twitchell for quite some time. And don't mind saying I never did cotton to him, either. He's a shrewd operator, and you never know what he's really thinking. Furthermore, he never lets go of a dollar until he's had a good feel of it. So he wouldn't have offered you fifteen hundred dollars to get rid of you without damned good cause. What's he got to fear from you?"

Allard turned his hands up. "You guess. I've tried

to and can't. He claimed he had his reasons, but he sure never showed any of his cards."

"Does he know you're interested in the old Kane range?"

"If he does he's a first-class mind reader as well as a banker."

"Beats me," rumbled Oglevie. "There's got to be an answer somewhere. We keep lookin', we may find it."

They rode along for some time, conversation dwindling as each sank back into his own privacy of thought. They breasted a long and gradual slope that crested off above the shallow sweep of a curving basin, down the center of which, between low banks of willow, a creek set up a wet and drowsy murmur.

But this peaceful sound was near-smothered and lost behind the bellowing complaint of cattle on the move, cattle being driven up through the basin, angling away from the creek toward the eastern crest almost directly in line with the spot where Frank Allard and Lafe Oglevie sat in their saddles.

"This is the place," said Oglevie. "This basin, and some more above and below and on the far side. This crest here marks the C Cross range limit. But those cattle coming through—just who in hell would be hazing stock in here? Unless Shark Knoles, or Jensen and Sevier, or Hub Stanley are shifting a sizable gather..."

"Who runs Durhams on the Bench?" cut in Allard on Oglevie's startled surmises. "Because there's a lot of Durham in that stuff coming through."

"You're right!" exclaimed Oglevie, standing high in his stirrups and staring. "And nobody on the Bench that I know of, runs Durhams. Man, what is this...?"

Allard had another keen-eyed survey of the approaching cattle before answering tersely. "There was a lot of Durhams in those last two shipping herds that went out of Pawnee. And both herds had rustling raids pulled on them. Maybe the answer to that is right here in front of us!"

Down by the creek a warning shout was a shrill summons above the protest of the cattle. A rider surged into view, breaking clear of the creek's willow covert. He pulled to a halt, staring up at the crest. Snake fast, he slithered from his saddle, dragging at a scabbarded rifle. Sunlight struck up a glinting shine on the weapon as he dropped to one knee and swung the gun into line.

Frank Allard whirled his roan from the crest while rapping out a harsh warning. "Look out, Lafe! Watch it—that fellow is cutting down on us!"

Lafe Oglevie was so thoroughly startled he was slow in reading the full significance of it all. He still held there, reared high in his saddle, staring. And then, even as he finally moved to haul his horse from the crest, that rifle down there snarled out its high, hard crash. There was a solid thud and Lafe Oglevie's horse flung a stricken head and went down in its tracks as though some unseen force had cut its legs from under it.

Lafe Oglevie had no chance to swing clear, for it all happened too fast. The weight of the horse came down heavily on the C Cross foreman's right leg. A bone snapped audibly and a gusty curse erupted from Oglevie's lips.

From the head of the fallen horse, almost squarely between the luckless animal's eyes, a thread of crimson began to seep.

CHAPTER TEN

FRANK ALLARD brought his rearing, startled roan to a spinning, hard-trampling stop, jumped from his saddle and, dragging at the reins, hauled over to where Lafe Oglevie lay. Hands spread against the earth, arms braced, Oglevie was fighting desperately to drag his trapped leg free of the dead weight of his stricken horse, all the while blurting his stunned and angry consternation.

"My leg, Frank! Busted. Felt it go—heard it go. What the hell have we bumped into? Who—why...?"

"No time for questions," cut in Allard bleakly. "We got to get out of here, and the first thing is to get you clear. So hang onto yourself and give me all you've got. Heave, now!"

Allard had his right arm around Lafe Oglevie's

shoulders, and with one booted foot braced against the bulk of the dead horse, hauled back with all his strength. Lafe Oglevie clawed the earth with spread fingers, jaw set with bitter grimness, the sweat of pain and savage effort beading out and trickling down his face and throat.

At first it seemed like a useless pull against something that would not yield one short inch. But these were two desperate men, each powerful in his own right, and now doubly so when spurred by stark necessity. They gained a little, then a little more, and abruptly the leg was free. But a boot had been left, trapped under the horse. And Lafe Oglevie's right leg, halfway between knee and ankle, swung loose and queerly twisted.

Propped on his sound left leg, Lafe Oglevie stared down at the broken one. "Goda'mighty, Frank—look at it. All crooked!"

"Shut up!" Allard's tone was savage with urgency. "Get into my saddle. I'll give you a hand. Pull yourself up!"

It was almost as bad as getting Oglevie loose from the dead horse, but they managed it, with the foreman pulling at horn and cantle and Allard lifting him.

The curving face of the crest in front of them had given them cover through these few frantic moments. Now Allard thrust the reins of the roan into Oglevie's hands and, crouching, moved back to the outer roll of the crest. "Got to have one more look, Lafe!"

He had his look, and it told him several things. The cattle were still coming on, pushed by a knot of riders at the drag. But now there was one rider out ahead of the cattle, spurring up the slope, rifle in hand.

Frank Allard, measuring the hard and unchangable factors of time, distance, and the range of a rifle over that of a handgun, saw immediately what he must try to do. Which was, by some means, get close enough to that rider to make the handgun effective. The angle of that onrushing rider was a little to one side and Allard, belt gun ready in his fist, moved to meet it, crouched and ready.

He was on one knee when the rider exploded across the crest. The man was reared slightly forward in his saddle, hat brim flattened back by the wind of progress, face predatory and eager and seeking. The fellow saw Lafe Oglevie first, now up on Allard's roan, and he was bringing his own mount to a sliding halt, rifle lifting to his shoulder, before he made out the crouched figure of Frank Allard, hardly more than fifteen yards to one side of him.

Instantly he understood that here was his real danger, and he tried to swing both horse and rifle to meet it. He got only partially around when Allard's gun bucked in recoil as it pounded out its report with a heavy finality.

The rider seemed to lift a little in his saddle as the big slug took him, then fell forward across the horn of his saddle, rifle sliding from his hand. For a short moment or two he hung that way, across the saddle horn and along his horse's neck. Then he poured limply to the ground, dragging the reins with him.

It wasn't much anchorage for a fretting, frantic horse, this dying man's grip on the reins. But it was all Frank Allard needed, for he was up and racing forward the moment he saw that his single shot had gone home. He lunged for the reins and caught them, just as their former owner's grip loosened.

Allard fought the rearing horse with harsh strength, bringing it under control. He caught up the dead man's rifle and lunged into the captured saddle. He whirled the horse, a sorrel, and yelled at Lafe Oglevie.

"Get out of here, Lafe—fast! Too many down there with the cattle for us to argue with. Ride for it!"

They tore away, heading for the nearest timber island that lay back along the way they had come. Allard put Oglevie and the roan out ahead of him and, as he rode, kept throwing glances over his shoulder to the rear. They made the shelter of the timber island, just as two more riders broke over the, up to now, sheltering crest.

Allard levered a couple of shots with the captured rifle, shooting to warn, rather than hit. And when the slugs dug up gouts of earth and whined by in ricochet, the two riders took the hint, and spun their mounts back across the curving crest.

Breaking for the far side of the timber, Allard urged Oglevie on. "Keep going, Lafe!"

But now, nothing more came after them, neither riders or the whisper and snap of searching lead. For one thing, the timber island was a barrier to hide their retreat for some distance, and afterward, by the time they had ridden clear of that cover, they had a running lead which could not be overtaken or reached by gunfire.

Knowing this, Allard spurred up beside Oglevie. The C Cross foreman rode heavy in the saddle now, jaw set, eyes pinched down, and one hand braced against the saddle horn to ease the shock of the roan's running. His broken leg swung limp outside the jouncing stirrup.

There was nothing Allard could do in any way to ease Lafe Oglevie's pain. This was a ride Lafe had to make on his own, all the way back to the C Cross headquarters. All Allard could do was keep beside him and watch the back trail.

"You can make it, Lafe?"

"I can make it. Frank, what did we bump into—what's it all about?"

"The answer to that will have to come later. All that matters now is to get you home."

They kept to a full run until the horses began to lather and labor in their stride. Then Allard cut the pace a little, watching Lafe Oglevie carefully. Wrapped in stoic, hard-jawed purpose, Lafe gave out no word of complaint, just rode steadily. Under the deep weather tan of his face, however, a trace of pallor was creeping. He had the look of a man who was drawing all the will and strength he knew into a harsh determination to stick the saddle and ride this thing out.

They scattered cattle along the way as they rode, cattle grazing or moving in toward timber islands to rest away from the sun, and many of the animals, after racing off to one side, would turn and stare in bovine wonder at these two riders dashing past.

Again Allard cut the pace, certain now there was no longer any pursuit to fear. A hundred questions were throbbing through his mind, but he put these all aside for later answering. First things first, and the first thing here was Lafe Oglevie and that twisted, broken leg.

As with all things, there was an end to time and distance, and so they finally came up to the C Cross headquarters. The hand forge in the corral was still going, and the two ranch hands working there at first stared, then came scrambling over the fence and hurrying up to the two lathered and run-out horses that came to a gusty stop at the bunkhouse door.

"What the hell?" came a demanding question. "What's the matter with Lafe?"

"Broken leg," answered Frank Allard briefly. "Bear a hand here—and easy!"

The questioner was suspicious, hostile. "Your fault, maybe? You led Lafe into something?"

"Shut up, Tyce!" growled Oglevie wearily. "Do as Allard says. Get me into my bunk."

They eased him out of the saddle, got their shoulders under his arms, and virtually carried him into the bunkhouse. They eased him down on a bunk, and when Allard, as gently as he could, cupped hands under the broken leg and lifted it to the blankets, the muscles of the foreman's jaw bunched and crawled and the sweat of acute agony slimed his face again. Oglevie's eyes closed and he let out a heavy sigh.

Over at the ranchhouse a screen door slammed, and then it was Barbara Chancellor who came hurrying into the bunkhouse.

"Lafe!" she cried. "What's happened to him?"

"Broken leg," Allard explained. "His horse fell on him. Doctor Sanchez will have to be brought out here, and from the look of things, he'll have a mean job ahead of him. Time counts. I'll get Doc. I could use a fresh horse. My roan's pretty well run out."

Barbara dropped on her knees by Oglevie's bunk, her mouth going soft and quivering. "Lafe!"

Oglevie's eyes opened and the glimmerings of the old leonine grin showed. He lifted a hand to her slim shoulder. "Clumsy old fool, that's me, youngster. Should have swung clear. Now don't you go gettin' all fussed up over me. It's only a busted leg, so, I'll be all right." Oglevie looked past the girl's head. "Tyce, either you or Del catch up a fresh bronc for Allard. Lark and the other boys still on that salting chore back on Grizzly?"

"Reckon so. They should be in any time now, though. Lafe, how'd your bronc happen to fall on you? And where is the horse?"

"Back on the edge of the old Kane place. Dead. Fell because it was shot." Oglevie closed his eyes again.

Allard headed off further questioning with a few curtly harsh explanations. "Lafe and I bumped into something shady. Some cattle coming up past Plume Creek, heading for the C Cross range. Lot of Durham stuff, like was in the last two herds to ship out of Pawnee. Both those herds had rustling raids pulled on them. Looks like what Lafe and I saw could be the rustled stock. Just why they're being pushed on to C Cross range, I wouldn't know—yet! But whoever was driving the cattle was put out enough on being caught at it to take a shot at us. They killed Lafe's horse. Now you know. Get that fresh bronc for me!"

The two cowhands went out. Barbara Chancellor got to her feet and faced Allard. She had changed from the riding togs she'd been wearing earlier in the day to a gingham housedress, and it made her look younger, more girlish. With her hair fluffed softly about her temples and her eyes moistly bright from the rush of emotion she'd known at Oglevie's mishap, she was very appealing.

"You're suggesting that there might be some kind of trouble ahead for this ranch?" she asked. "What could it be?"

"That I don't know—not for sure." Allard told her gravely. "But as soon as I get Doc Sanchez started on his way out here, I'll do what I can to find out. I suggest as soon as your other riders come in, that you hold them pretty close to headquarters for a time. I'll see that you get the word if I uncover anything that shapes up as a real threat to the C Cross. Lafe, anything I can do for you besides getting Doc Sanchez?"

"Yeah," rumbled Lafe. "This. Any time it strikes you as real necessary, throw that badge away and take over here. Tyce and Del and the rest are all good men, but they need a steady head to run things."

"No!" Barbara Chancellor exclaimed. "That isn't necessary. I can—."

"No, you can't, girl," headed off Oglevie. "Frank—ah—well, we left a dead man back there where the trouble broke. It had to be that way, because it was his scalp or ours. And when any shootin' trouble breaks, then it's business for men. Frank, can I depend on you?"

Allard nodded. "You can, Lafe. All the way."

From the door, Tyce called. "That fresh bronc is ready."

Allard paused for a final look at Barbara. "If there's whiskey on the place, give him some. He's got something real rough to look forward to and to live with. I'll make things as fast as possible. Stay with it, Lafe...!"

He turned and hurried out.

Barbara Chancellor stared at the empty doorway for a moment before turning back to Lafe Oglevie.

"You say you—you left a dead man back there, Lafe. Did—did Frank Allard—?"

"Yeah," Oglevie told her quietly. "Frank got him. The way things had shaped up, I couldn't do anything about it. So, if Frank hadn't got him, then neither of us would have ridden back to this ranch. Tough man, Frank Allard. Tough a man as I ever met up with. But it's the right kind of toughness, so don't you get proud or stubborn, Barbara. If Frank Allard has to take over here, you just go along with the fact and don't try and clutter up things. Just be thankful there's one like him to take hold of the rope. Now, youngster—I could stand a good jolt of that liquor..."

In the back room of the Palace, Haley Twitchell paced nervously up and down, chewing his soggy cigar. At the center table, bottle and glass in front of him, Pinto Jardene sat. There was a faint flush on his smooth, dark cheeks and his eyes were hard and shiny. There was a faint, musing smile on his lips, giving him the look of a man imbued with a deep, inner excitement, an almost feverish anticipation, and liking it. The look of a born gambler, perhaps, with the biggest bet of his life riding on a single card, and impatient for that card to be turned. He drummed his fingers on the table.

Haley Twitchell paused in his nervous pacing and spoke heavily. "I don't like it, Pinto. It's wrong—wrong because it won't work. We're pulling down our world around our ears."

Jardene's voice ran soft, but biting. "Damn a man who wants to hedge on a bet! Twitchell, where are your guts—or haven't you got any? We've been over all this before. Once it was a fine idea, a great idea. You were all for it—just couldn't wait for the wheels to start rolling. We couldn't miss, so you claimed. Yeah, you were all for it, plenty! Now you're starting to crawl. For God's sake, why?"

Twitchell came around to face the dive owner. "I've

told you why a dozen times. Just one word says it all. Allard, Frank Allard! I've had a feeling about men before, and I've been right. I've got that feeling about Allard."

"One man," scoffed Jardene. "And mortal. You'll see."

"Yes, just one man," said Twitchell. "But one man, if he's the right man, can anchor a hundred others. Whole empires have been held together and saved by one man. What luck have we had so far in getting rid of Allard? None, not a damn bit. Once he got that badge, we couldn't fire him for the simple reason he wouldn't stand for being fired. So you tried Harry Shelline, and how far did he get? I tried to buy Allard off, and—"

"You what?" exploded Jardene as he came halfway out of his chair, leaning across the table, mouth twisted, eyes raging.

Haley Twitchell, in his fervor of argument, had let his tongue get away from him and had said more than he intended to. But he'd said it, and now there was no use trying to cover up. He gave back a little under the impact of Jardene's fierce glare, then shrugged with a trace of the heavy sulkiness that was so much a part of his son's makeup.

Pinto Jardene pounded the table with a clenched fist. "You mean to tell me you were stupid enough to offer Allard money? Money if he'd do what?"

"Money if he'd blow the country—ride out and not come back," blurted the banker. "What's so stupid about that?"

"How much did you offer him?"

"Fifteen hundred dollars. I'd have gone higher, if he'd shown any signs of willingness to talk business. But he wouldn't even listen."

Pinto Jardene came fully to his feet, shoving his chair back to violently upset it and filled the room with a hard clatter.

"You fool!" Jardene raged. "You damned, lily-livered

fool! Why didn't you really let your hair down? Why didn't you write our whole plan down on a piece of paper for him, so he'd really know what was in the wind? Up to now I figured you really did have at least a few brains, maybe a smidgen of them! I was wrong, for you haven't. You haven't got the brains of the dumbest sheep that ever walked!"

Twitchell's sulkiness grew, and the tongue-lashing Pinto Jardene threw at him roused a flare of defiance in reply.

"I don't see where you've been so damn smart, Jardene. Harry Shelline was going to take care of everything, wasn't he? Oh, yes, he was a cinch to take care of Allard. Just so—just so! Allard was as good as dead and buried, once you turned Shelline loose on him. Well, who's dead and buried now, and who's alive and walking tall? My method of trying to get rid of Allard might have been different than yours, and if it didn't work, well, neither did yours. So what are you doing all the shouting for?"

Now it was Jardene's turn to pace the room while he spoke with a biting harshness. "The angle of getting rid of Allard, or not getting rid of him, is not what I'm talking about. It's what those attempts could have told him. Shelline's try for him told him nothing beyond the fact that a man he'd given a floater to, had slipped back into town to make a try at gulching him from the dark. Even if he figures that I did set Shelline after him doesn't tell him anything for sure, either. For he knows I hate him clear past hell for personal reasons, if not for anything else. But you—with your stupid attempt to buy him off, that can tell him anything—and everything!"

"I don't see how it can," defended Twitchell. "He don't know but what—"

Pinto Jardene swung to a stop not a stride from Twitchell, and now he lifted an arm, and jabbed a taut forefinger against the banker's chest, jabbing with it again and again to emphasize his biting words.

"How you ever made the money you have, I'll be damned if I know. Listen, you fool—here's what your offer of runout money to Allard told him, and why. It told him that there was some kind of big deal in the air. It told him that it was our kind of a deal, not his, and for that reason we didn't want him to be around to mix in and maybe clutter up the works.

"Why did it tell him that? Because you had no legitimate reason for wanting to get rid of him. Oh, maybe you don't like him, and he knows it. Probably he don't like you, either. But there's been no open fight between you, and little chance that there would be. Yet you offer him fifteen hundred dollars to get out of Pawnee, out of this part of the country, and to stay gone. It didn't work. But here's what it did do. It started him thinking—it must have. It started him asking questions of himself. And when you start a man to doing that, you never know when he's liable to come up with the right answer. Now can you get that through your skull?"

Haley Twitchell backed away from that jabbing finger. Inside he was quaking, not from physical fear of Pinto Jardene, but because the dive owner's words were bringing aloud possibilities that had been haunting Haley Twitchell from the moment Frank Allard had turned down the runout money. However, there was still enough bluster in Twitchell for him to try and justify himself.

"I figured I was on safe ground, Pinto. Who'd ever think that a damned down-and-out drifter would pass up fifteen hundred dollars—easy dollars? A fifth of that much, or less, has bought more than one man's death. All Allard had to do to earn it was hit the trail and keep on drifting. I tell you—"

Jardene waved him to silence. "No—I'm telling you! Your trouble, Twitchell, is that you see everything in terms of money, and you're blind to everything else. Should a doctor ever have to cut you open, he'll find that your insides consist of yellow blubber wrapped around a thousand-dollar bank note. Well, I like money, myself—lots of it. But I've seen enough of human nature to know that there are some who are crazy enough to put other things, such as fanciful ideas about so-called honor and self-respect, ahead of any amount of money. Now, anybody with half an eye should have seen that Frank Allard was one of that crazy kind— one of those proud buckos who figure it's smart to die, rather than duck. And though I hate him as I've hated few men, I'll give him this due. He's smart—smart enough to ask questions and to find out the answers. And you, you fumbling fool, you tipped our hand. Arh-h-h!"

Jardene swung an arm in supreme disgust, turned to the table, poured a stiff shot of whiskey, and downed it at a gulp.

The forlorn heaviness came back to Haley Twitchell. "All right," he blurted. "Say I made a mistake. There's no use making another and bigger one by trying to go through with the deal. Let's call it off and forget it, all around."

Pinto Jardene dropped back in his chair and the low, raging note again thickened his voice. "Call it off! Why you driveling, spineless idiot—how can we? By this time Ned Fargo and his boys have pushed those stolen cattle well in onto the C Cross range. I've talked to Starke and Harper and sold them on the idea that the C Cross is the outfit that stole their cattle and killed one of Starke's men. I've told them they'd find the proof in their cattle running with the C Cross cows on the C Cross range. The whole deal as we first figured it has been all worked out and put on the move. So answer me this. How in hell can we call it off?"

Haley Twitchell had no answer to this, and Jardene,

after biting the tip off a cigar with a snap of his teeth, went on.

"I'd look good, wouldn't I, calling Starke and Harper back in here and telling them it was all a mistake, and that I had no idea where their cows were or who had rustled them? Of course they'd believe me. Oh, yes— like hell they would! I'd look good trying to unravel a lot of strings I've braided into a play for the biggest pot of my life. Well, we're not calling anything off. We're going through with it. We're going to ride our luck, have a look at the cards. And if the luck turns bad, don't ever think you're going to slip out a side door and leave me holding the sack. For that would be the biggest mistake you ever made—and the last. The men who've tried to double-cross Pinto Jardene are all dead! Something for you to remember, Twitchell. Now get out of here! I turn sick looking at you."

The banker did not argue or object. He moved heavily to the door and went through it, and under the staining tobacco slime, his coarse lips were pallid and unsteady.

Con Waters had his fastest team harnessed to a buckboard, and now he sat, gaunt and angular on the buckboard seat. With set brake and taut reins, he held the fretting team steady while waiting for Doc Sanchez to come from his office with his satchel and other necessary gear.

Frank Allard stood beside the buckboard, face hard and thoughtful under a hat brim pulled low to ward off in part the flat blaze of a rapidly westering sun. He'd been talking tersely to Con, and now, as he waited for Con's reply, he twisted up a cigarette. Con spoke with the slowness of a man searching through puzzled thoughts.

"In a way it don't make a lick of sense, Frank. Why would men go to all the risk of rustling a jag on cattle from a couple of trail herds and then drive the stock onto the range of a big, established cattle outfit, where the rustled stuff was sure to be found? Men steal cattle for the same reason they steal other things of value— so as to profit in what they think is the easy way. Why, a man asks himself—why—? Unless—" Con went silent, a sharp glint beginning to spark in his eyes.

"Unless what, Con?" asked Allard.

"Unless the rustlers wanted the stock to be found by the rightful owner of the animals, and on that particular piece of range. Like this, for instance." Con cleared his throat, while his eyes pinched down as he marshaled his thoughts. "Say I have a grudge against another man for some reason. I want to do him harm without showing my hand. So I steal a horse and smuggle the animal into this man's stable. Then by one means or another I see that word gets to the rightful owner of the horse just where it might be found. The owner investigates, finds the horse, and calls the owner of the stable to account as a horse thief."

Frank Allard nodded slowly. "I've considered that same line of thought," he admitted. "But who would have it in for the C Cross?"

"That is a question I find hard to answer," Con admitted. At this moment Doc Sanchez hove into sight, hurrying. Con straightened and shifted his grip on the reins. "But maybe this is the line we should be thinking along. The C Cross is the biggest and richest spread on the Bench. And from the beginnings of time, men have been known to covet that which is big and rich."

Doc Sanchez, panting a little, put his satchel and an armful of assorted other gear under the buckboard seat before climbing up beside Con.

"Give us a real job, Doc," Allard said. "Lafe Oglevie is one first-class man."

Con Waters kicked off the brake, slacked up a little on the reins. The eager team surged into their collars and the buckboard skittered away, made the turn at the street junction, and scudded on into the lifting grade of the Bench trail.

Gil Paxton came out on the porch of the store, lifted a beckoning hand. Allard crossed over.

"What's taking Doc Sanchez up on the Bench in such a hurry?" Paxton asked.

"Horse fell on Lafe Oglevie," reported Allard briefly. "Broke Lafe's leg."

Allard did not elaborate, nor know any desire to. For of late Gil Paxton had become increasingly hard to talk to. A change had come over the man. No longer was he easy and genial in his manner. Now there was a hardness in him, a bruskness, and something far back in his eyes that warded a man off and held him at a distance.

Nell Kane came out onto the porch, moved to the edge of it, where the slanting glow of nearing sunset could touch her. She looked at Allard and, though her lips showed a faint smile, there was a strained uneasiness in her manner. Gil Paxton spoke sharply and without turning.

"Nell, you get on inside! Time to be thinking of supper."

Allard watched the rebellion flare up in the girl. "I've been inside all day. I've the right to—"

"You'll do as I say," cut in Paxton harshly. "I'll not have you out here showing yourself to these damned trail herd cowhands. Where's your sense of shame? I think you like to have them staring at you."

For a moment the rebellion seemed about to flare higher. Then there was a swift misting of the girl's eyes and her lips trembled. "That—that isn't true. You've no right to say such things. I—"

"Get inside!"

It was almost as though Paxton had wielded a whip. The girl shrank back, then with lowered head and dragging step went into the store. Paxton turned to follow her, but paused as Frank Allard's words hit out at him savagely.

"Just a minute, Paxton—just a minute! What the

goddamn hell's the matter with you, acting that way toward a kid like Nell—treating her like she was a dog. Anybody would think you figured her a slave. Well, she's not. Have you gone completely crazy?"

Gil Paxton met Allard's angry gaze with a sort of deep indrawing that left his face wooden, his eyes strangely blank. "Know what I'm doing, Allard. All my affair. You stay out of it."

Allard gave it back to him, just as bluntly. "Stay out, hell! There's an item of business I want to talk over with Nell Kane, and I'll be around one of these days to do that very thing. And after I get through talking with Nell, then I'll have something to say to you, too. Some questions I figure to ask you, Paxton—one in particular. About somebody running down the street when there wasn't anybody running down the street."

If Allard hoped to get some sort of reaction out of Gil Paxton with these statements, he was disappointed. For the stoniness of the storekeeper's expression did not change in the slightest; it was like looking at a blank wall. And Paxton spoke no word, either. He just turned away and walked solidly into the store.

Frank Allard, still simmering but knowing also a stifling sense of futility, headed for the office. The sun, which had seemingly hung in indecision just above the western rim of the world, now plunged abruptly into a sea of scarlet fire. And then twilight's misting was a flowing tide that poured along the street and crawled up the sides of buildings and began spreading an all-engulfing shadow up the lifting slope of the Bench.

CHAPTER ELEVEN

LEE MOSBY put aside the somewhat tattered magazine he'd been glancing through, leaned far back in his chair, stretched his arms wide, and hugely yawned.

"Where the devil you been, Frank? Thought for a while you might be sleeping in for the day, but when I talked to Ben Ripon he said you'd been up and on the move by noon. Made an afternoon of it somewhere, eh?"

Allard nodded brusquely. "Call it that." His fingers worked at the bent and battered badge on his shirt, got it free, and laid it on the desk. "Giving it back, Lee. I'm quitting you."

The front legs of Mosby's tipped-back chair hit the floor with a thump as he straightened abruptly and leaned forward. "Quitting me! What's the idea? Man, you're nothing if not sudden."

Allard pulled up a chair, built another smoke, his face a hard mask in the room's deepening shadow.

"I'm waiting," murmured Mosby. "And wondering why?"

Allard lit his cigarette. "Things I got to do—out from behind the shelter of the badge. The badge stands for something that could tie my hands, and I don't want them tied. So—" He shrugged.

"I'm listening," Mosby said, "if you care to talk."

"Why not?" Allard said. He went on to tell the story of the afternoon, up on the Bench. Mosby whistled softly and in effect, almost repeated Con Waters' exact words.

"Worst mixed-up mess I ever heard of. Don't make sense."

"Yes and no," Allard admitted. "But it sets a man to asking questions of himself, and when he asks enough of them, even though he comes up minus a lot of answers, he still manages to get the hazy beginnings of a possible picture. Consider this. A couple of times you've mentioned to me that you'd been puzzling some about those rustling raids, about who could have pulled them and where the cattle would be driven to and held and eventually disposed of. You also said you had a hunch that the two herd owners, Abel Starke and Brack Harper, were cooking up something. Well, add those things to these."

Allard went on to tell of seeing Starke and Harper in some kind of conference with Pinto Jardene in the back room of the Palace. He also told of Haley Twitchell's try at buying him off for fifteen hundred dollars. "Add all that to what Lafe Oglevie and I bumped into this afternoon up on the Bench, and what answer do you get?"

"I can't think that fast," said Mosby. "But you must figure you got an answer, or you wouldn't be turning in your badge. I'm all mithered down, and I admit it. What really whips me is Haley Twitchell offering you fifteen hundred dollars to leave town and you being fool enough to turn it down. If he'd offered it to me, I'd have—"

"Done just what I did," cut in Allard. "Told him to go to hell."

"I wonder!" exclaimed Mosby. Then after a short period of silence he added gruffly, "Well, maybe I would have, right now. But if Twitchell had put that kind of money in front of me not so long ago, back when I'd forgotten I was a man, I'd probably have jumped at it. But why that offer to you, Frank—why?"

"The first night you and I met, after I'd been hired on as your night man, you and I had a little talk right here where we're sitting now, if you remember." Allard paused long enough to flip the butt of his smoked out cigarette through the open door. "Among other things," he went on, "we discussed the various citizens of Pawnee and how much weight they carried. I asked you about young Royce Twitchell. You told me he was just a spoiled, sarcastic pup who didn't rate a thing. You also said that his chief activity in life was paying court to Barbara Chancellor with his father's full approval. You added that if Royce and Barbara made a match of it, that would give the Twitchells control of the C Cross and set them up in great fashion on the Bench. Well, you could have been hitting the nail on the head, Lee—only you wouldn't know then that maybe there was some sort of deal in the works to make damn sure of getting hold of the C Cross. Because maybe Royce wasn't doing too well in playing for Miss Chancellor's favor. When you look at things from that angle, then this and that begin to jell a little, don't you think?"

"More than a little," agreed Mosby. "Go on, man—go on!"

"Remember, I'm supposing a lot," cautioned Allard. "I'm guessing this way and that, without a smidgen of real proof. Maybe I'll come up with real proof later. I sure aim to try. We'll say that Haley Twitchell wants the C Cross. When it begins to look like his son's chances of marrying it aren't so good at all, friend Twitchell figures another angle. He wants to hide his hand until he can safely show it. So he has this Ned Fargo *hombre* and his crowd of wild ones stage a couple of rustling raids on trail herds coming up from the south. Naturally the owners of the herds are all frothed up over the raids, and they'd like to get the stolen cattle back, while at the same time knocking all hell out of whoever did the rustling."

Lee Mosby slapped a hand on the table. "Now you're really getting somewhere—now the light begins to filter through even my thick head, and I get the rest. Which is that the rustled stock are pushed on to the C Cross range and a hint is laid down where Abel Starke and Brack Harper can't miss finding it. So they investigate and find their stolen cattle running on the C Cross range along with the C Cross critters. Natural conclusion is that the C Cross did the rustling. Starke and Harper call in their crews to really work the C Cross over. When the smoke clears away, the C Cross is weakened down to where Twitchell can take over."

"Twitchell—and Pinto Jardene," Allard said harshly. "Remember that I saw Starke and Harper with their heads damned close together with Jardene in the back room of the Palace. Twitchell and Jardene are like that." Allard held up his hand, first and second fingers pressed close together. "I can't see Twitchell in this without Jardene, for Fargo is one of Jardene's men. So it's got to be Twitchell and Jardene."

"I go along with that," Mosby said. "It makes sense."

"The Bench," Allard mused aloud, "is a big stretch of range country, plenty big, and rich in all the things that make for valuable cattle country, grass, water, and timber enough for shelter, winter or summer. A cattle empire, if a man had it all to himself. Now, if the wrong kind of people had control of the C Cross, how much trouble would they have squeezing out all the smaller outfits on the Bench?"

"Damn little," agreed Mosby succinctly. "No, not much trouble at all, not if they wanted to get real tough about it. And with that kind of a head start, I can see Jardene and Twitchell coming up real tough, because they'd have Ned Fargo and his crowd to do the fighting and necessary rough stuff for them. Frank, if I had a pin handy I'd stick myself with it, to see if this isn't all a bad and wild dream."

"No dream, Lee. Just a hard and ugly fact, becoming more solid all the time." Allard got to his feet, took a turn up and down the office. "The only angle I find hard to fit in is Twitchell's try at buying me off. Yeah, that has me fighting my head."

"Maybe I can answer that for you," Mosby said. "The night we got Twitchell and Jardene to agree in hiring you on as a night man for me, they saw you as just another sheep like I was at that time. And like Jardene said—if you didn't creep and crawl before them, they could always fire you. But things didn't work out that way. Turned out you didn't fire easy. In fact, you didn't fire at all. You ran Shelline out of town and slapped Jardene down. You lit a fire under me. You faced up to Lafe Oglevie and the C Cross, and then made friends with them. When Shelline sneaked back into town and tried to get you from the dark, it was you who got him and—."

"Lucky there," Allard growled. "Just plain damn fool lucky."

"Some luck, maybe, but not all," Mosby went on. "Lot of guts and straight shooting, too. So, all up and down the line you came up too tough to fire, too tough to scare, and in the showdown with Shelline, just too damn tough to kill. So you had them running scared. There was only one other way to try and get rid of you, which was to buy you off. Only, that didn't work, either. Yes, sir, man—I think that would be the answer."

"Makes me out a hell of a lot bigger man than I am," Allard objected. "But we'll let it go as such. Now I

177

wonder—where do you think I might find this Brack Harper if I can't locate him here in town?"

"From what I hear, his outfit is camped out west of town a little way," Mosby directed. "What you want him for?"

"Like this," Allard said slowly. "I had a pretty fair look at him when I saw him in that back room with Starke and Jardene. And I kind of liked what I saw. Lee, he's a different breed than Starke, who's got a mean, pigheaded streak in him. But this Brack Harper, while he shaped up as being plenty salty as I judged him, also struck me as a man I could talk to. I aim to have a try at him, anyhow."

Allard moved to the door. Lee Mosby picked up the battered badge. "Damn!" he swore. "I don't like to see you without this badge, Frank. We had the makings of a pretty stout pair, you and me."

"Still have," said Allard. "I'll be around, fellah."

There were a couple of worn and battered trail wagons pulled up side by side. Just off the end of one of them a fire burned close to the earth, spiking the dark with a small cone of ruddy radiance. A man with an old flour sack for an apron was active about the flames, and the warm, good, enticing odors of readying food drifted across the night. Faintly touched by the widest reach of the firelight, men squatted on their heels or lounged at length against the well-grassed sod. From a few yards out, Frank Allard lifted his quiet hail.

"Hello there, at the fire!"

There was a little stir and a short interval of silence before an answer came, curt and brief.

"Come on in!"

He could feel the impact of men's glances and their fixed attention as he strode up. The moment the firelight limned him fully, there was a muffled exclamation.

"It's that bucko night marshal!"

"He's got no authority outside of town," said another. "And we're out!"

"Not trying to bring any authority," assured Allard quietly. "Just want to have a little confab with Brack Harper. He around?"

One of the squatting figures straightened up. "Right here. What can I do for you?" The words were curt and crisp and a little wary perhaps, yet not entirely hostile.

"Like I said, a little talk with you," answered Allard. "Worth your time, I think."

"My boys haven't stirred up any trouble," Harper said. "Nobody in town can complain."

"Nobody is complaining," Allard told him. "This is about something else. And all friendly."

Brack Harper seemed satisfied. "All right," he said, and led the way out past the wagons, where he paused and turned. "Well?"

"It's about the cattle you had rustled off you. Interested?"

"Hell yes—of course! What about the cattle?"

Allard twisted up a smoke. "It's quite a story," he said. "Some things I know for certain, some I'm guessing at. I'm hoping you may be able to furnish answers to some of the guesses."

"One little question, first," said Brack Harper bluntly. "Why should you be interested? Not your cattle."

"True enough," Allard nodded. "Suppose we call it the element of right or wrong. Together with a matter of friendship with some. Such things enter, you know."

"Fair enough," Brack Harper admitted. "Go ahead."

Allard did so, once again telling of the happenings of the afternoon. Brack Harper listened without speaking, though toward the end he began stirring restlessly. But not until Allard was done did the cattleman speak, and when he did it was harshly.

"Mister, either you, or somebody else is lying like hell!"

"Not me," returned Allard quietly, with no show of

offence. "Because I can take you out to the C Cross headquarters and show you Lafe Oglevie tied to his bunk with a broken leg. Also, I can take you to the spot where Lafe and I ran into trouble, and somewhere around there I'll show you Lafe's dead horse. The crowd who were driving in the stock can pack off the fellow I had to gun, but they can't do much about a dead horse. They might try to drag it off someplace, but that would leave an easy trail to follow. So, friend, I can prove every word I've spoken." On a sudden hunch, he added, "Can Pinto Jardene do as much?"

He sensed Brack Harper's slight start of surprise. "What's Pinto Jardene got to do with it?"

Allard pinched out the stub of his cigarette and tossed it aside. "This," he said, "is where I start to guess. Tell me if I come close. I'd guess that Jardene has told you and Abel Starke where you could find your rustled stock. Which would be on the C Cross range. I'd guess he probably added quite a considerable amount of coloring to that statement, to sort of suggest that the C Cross was a big, bad outfit, ready to figure that any and all trail herds were fair game any time the opportunity came along for them to pull a raid and get away with it. I'd guess that Jardene painted the Bench as a big chunk of country, which it certainly is, with a lot of wild back reaches where a lot of rustled stock could be held and pretty well-hidden—which also is true, too. But if Jardene told you and Abel Starke that the C Cross stole your cattle, he lied in his teeth. And if he sold you and Starke on the idea of going up on the Bench with your combined crews, for the purpose of smashing the C Cross, as well as getting back your rustled stock, then you're a bigger fool than I judged you to be."

Allard's tone had chilled as he went along, and his words were harsh when he finished.

Brack Harper kept silent for a little time while he put together a smoke. And when he flicked a match alight and touched the flame to his cigarette, the small flare disclosed a lean, deeply weathered face, just now fixed with grim thought. Harper waved the match back and forth to extinguish it, then threw it aside.

"For a guesser," he admitted, "you're doing one very hell of a job. But suppose you give me an answer. What's Jardene got against the C Cross? Why would he want the outfit smashed?"

"So that he and others in on his scheme could move in and take over," Allard said. "You haven't been up on the Bench yet, have you? Well, it's big country and as fine a cattle range as I ever saw. The C Cross is the very heart of it, the big power. If a man owned the C Cross and was of a mind to, he could squeeze out all the smaller outfits up there, and have the whole thing to himself—a virtual empire."

"And that, you believe, would be Jardene's long-term program?" Harper queried.

"Just about. It'll do until a better hunch comes along."

"One more question," Harper pressed. "Have you spoken like this to Abel Starke?"

Allard shook his head. "No," he said flatly, "I haven't. You see, Abel Starke don't like me. For that matter, I doubt there's much in the world that he does like, for the man's got a sour streak in him. I had to pull him and a few of his crew up pretty short when they first hit town and ran a little wild. At that time Starke was understandably sore over the rustling raid that had been pulled against him, and because of that, wanted to take out his mad on the town of Pawnee as a whole. I had to head him off. I came to you tonight because from what I'd seen of you, you struck me as a fair man and one who has his feet on the ground. I still think I'm right in that judgment."

Again Brack Harper was silent for a little time, sucking on his cigarette, the tip alternately glowing, then fading. When he did speak, it was slowly. "I try to be fair, because it's good sense as well as comforting to the conscience. And," here his tone crisped, "I do purely hate to be taken for a sucker. And friend, as far as Pinto Jardene is concerned, you've hit the nail squarely on the head. All that you said he probably told Starke and me, is just about exactly what he did tell us. He's got Starke completely sold, but I got to admit that, while I was willing to listen to him, I didn't swallow the bait at one gulp. I'd made up my mind to reserve judgment all along the line and to act accordingly."

Frank Allard let out a small sigh of relief. "Good man! I knew I'd guessed you right."

"Understand, of course," said Harper, "I don't take kindly to being rustled anymore than the next, and I'll string a cow thief just as quickly as the next. But as for being a sucker and pulling another's chestnuts out of the fire at the risk of my own neck and those of my men—no, thanks!"

"But you were going up on the Bench for a call on the C Cross?" Allard asked.

"Tomorrow morning," admitted Harper. "Starke was all for hitting the C Cross tonight, catching them off guard and really cleaning house. I told him that didn't go for me and that if he wanted to try it that way, he'd have to go it alone. So he agreed to wait until tomorrow."

"But you meant it just now when you said you'd string a cow thief as quickly as the next man?" Allard queried.

"Every damn word!" Harper rapped. "If I'd been able to believe Jardene without any reservations, I'd be riding with Starke tonight. Because that raid on my herd has cost me a chunk of money, even should I get the cattle back. It's like this. I lost too many to just write them off and forget. Yet there's not enough of them to justify the expense of ordering up three or four cars and shipping them, because transporting beef stock by railroad doesn't come exactly cheap. So either I go to the time and bother to drive them clear back to their home range again, or I sell them at a sacrifice to some local outfit. So it comes up that whichever way I move I lose money. Yes, sir, mister—show me those really responsible for that raid and I'll sure as hell make them hard to catch!"

"I might," murmured Allard, "be able to do that very thing—show you the thieves, I mean. That's providing you'd make a little night ride with me, out to Plume Creek. For I understand that a certain Ned Fargo and several of his wild ones got a camp out there. It's also known that this Ned Fargo has been run off other ranges for being too free and easy with other people's cattle. Also, Fargo is friendly enough with Pinto Jardene to sit with him and others at poker games in Jardene's back room. Considering these facts, it isn't too hard to put two and two together, don't you think?"

"No, it isn't," agreed Brack Harper, "not too hard at all." He was quietly thoughtful for a moment or two, a man sorting out his thoughts before going on musingly, speaking those thoughts aloud. "The way you add things up it comes out something like this. That Pinto Jardene has this Fargo and his crowd raid Starke and me, and push the rustled stuff on to the C Cross range. After which he gives Starke and me a cock-and-bull story about the C Cross and hints that we'll probably find our cattle on the C Cross range. We take a look and there they are, sure enough. So then we take it out on the C Cross and cut them down to virtually nothing, which would make it easy, after Starke and I pull out, for Jardene and this fellow Fargo and his crowd to move in and take over. We do the dirty work and Jardene ends up owning himself a cattle empire. Well, well! Quite an ambitious scheme, for a fact. But then there's a logical side to your reasoning that's a lot more convincing than the line Jardene put out. So you know, friend—I'm of a mind to take that little ride with you, out to Plume Creek."

"Tonight?"

"Tonight!"

"A deal!" exclaimed Allard. "And if things shape up that Jardene is right and I'm wrong, you've got my permission to swing me as a cow thief."

Harper gave a soft, short laugh. "A chore I doubt I'll have to take on, Allard. What time tonight?"

"Couple of hours from now. I'll be out. I suggest you hold your boys here in camp. And I don't think there'd be any point in telling Starke about this, seeing he's already got his mind in a different groove."

"That makes sense, too," agreed Harper. "Be seeing you."

CHAPTER TWELVE

THEY PUSHED along steadily, a compact group of ten riders, with Frank Allard and Brack Harper out in front. Over a still, far-reaching world the stars sparkled and glistened. To the left, the lift of the Bench was a curve of masking blackness, while on the right all the earth was just a flat-running shadow, seemingly without limit.

As he rode, a keen tide of exultation surged in Frank Allard, as stronger and stronger grew the conviction that he was supremely right in all his calculations and reasoning and surmises. Things, he thought, generally worked out that way if a man put enough hard, logical reasoning into the problem. The actions of all men were invariably guided by their motives, whether good or bad. And once you garnered a fair answer to a motive, then the tangle of trails unwound and a man knew where he was going. There were answers to a number of things out ahead, and Allard was eager to come up with them.

An hour short of midnight they struck Plume Creek, a full two miles below where it left the slope of the Bench to cut a more leisurely way across the flatter plain, the moisture of its waters feeding ragged banks of willows and taller clumps of alders. They let their horses drink at a chuckling shallows, then crossed on over.

"If they're watching any side, it will be the side toward town," Allard said. "So we'll work up careful on this side. My guess is that their camp will be pretty well up toward the Bench."

"Fair enough," Harper agreed.

They rode at a walk now, and the black shoulders of the Bench lifted high and higher as they moved closer to it. There was a small night wind sliding down off the heights, and it pushed against their faces while carrying the muffled mutter of their horses' hoofs back and away below them. Frank Allard was hoping that it might help in another way, and abruptly it did. It brought to their nostrils the acrid tang of wood smoke.

Allard hauled up and spoke softly. "We try to ride all the way in, they're bound to hear us. And if possible, complete surprise is what we want."

Harper answered by swinging from his saddle, kneeling and taking off his spurs. He gave out a low order.

"Hap Jenkins will stay with the horses. Rest of you hang your spurs on your saddles and come along—soft!"

So they went on afoot, still outside the fringe of willow and alder growth, running down the trail of that betraying thread of wood smoke, watching carefully ahead for some show of the fire that was the source of it. Presently they located this, just the faintest diffusion of ruddy reflection against the all-pervading blackness of the night. They closed in with increasing stealth and care.

At some time in a distant past, a shoulder of hardpan bedrock had forced a division of Plume Creek's freshet waters. It had also fashioned a pocketing eddy wherein silt had settled and built gradually up. Succeeding years with their freshets had added to this until a small island had formed. On either side of the island wild waters had gouged still deeper channels, in effect lifting the island crest steadily higher. Now that island had become a long, narrow flat, encircled with creek growth for the most part. It was on the lower end of this flat that Ned Fargo's camp was thrown.

On the crest of a fifteen-foot cut bank, Frank Allard and Brack Harper sprawled flat and studied the layout. The fire had burned low, edged now with a margin of gray ash, the heart of it ruby-red with glowing coals. Two men hunkered down within reach of the fire's faint and fading radiance. Farther up the flat, horses stamped an occasional hoof as they shifted positions against night's deepening chill.

Harper touched Allard's elbow and his whisper was wind soft.

"Must be more than two of them."

"Are," Allard answered in kind. "Back from the fire where we can't see them."

The setup was far from satisfactory for Allard's purpose. As there was no way to tell just how many made up the rustler gang, and no way to place their position. A single lunge could carry the two by the fire into the safety of darkness. This thing would take some figuring.

Abruptly one of the visible men stood up, seemed to be listening. Then his curt remark carried clear. "Somebody ridin' in, Ned!"

The second figure by the fire hit his feet, stood gaunt and bony and bleakly alert. Coldly harsh, he directed his order into the dark beyond the fire. "Watch yourselves, out there! This could be word from Pinto. But you never know—so watch yourselves!" Here was Ned Fargo, a man wolf-wary, he was moving as he spoke, as was the man beside him. Now the dark held them, too.

By this time Frank Allard had picked up the sound of approaching hoofs. At Allard's elbow, Brack Harper whispered. "Missed our chance. Now we got to wait this thing out."

The nearing hoofs struck up the rattle of gravel, and then it was Ned Fargo's voice again, cutting cold across the night.

"Far enough. Where you ridin'?"

There was a guttural roughness in the answer that came back. "Lookin' for Ned Fargo's camp. This it?"

"Maybe. Why you lookin'?"

"Pinto Jardene sent me. Got word for Fargo."

There was a short, suspicious silence before Fargo said, "Come on in—but damn slow and careful. And you sure better be tellin' the truth!"

Now there was considerable movement, which Allard could hear but could not see—men shifting around, their voices a broken murmur. Hoofs moving in slowly, then stopping, and spur chains jangling faintly as a rider stepped from his saddle.

"Build up that fire," came Fargo's harsh order. "Want me a better look at this fellow."

Now figures began to show against the fire's dimming glow. Then added wood smoldered, caught, and flames began to lift and crackle. The circle of light widened, threw all things into brighter relief. Fargo came into the light, a thickset figure beside him.

Frank Allard heard Brack Harper draw a little hissing breath of surprise, and he gripped Harper's arm to silence him. For Allard had his own start of surprise. That burly figure at Fargo's side was Blackie Burke, Abel Starke's segundo!

A voice growled, "Watch him, Ned! He's a stranger to me."

"With me, too," answered Fargo. "So—I'm wonderin'."

There was a cockiness in Blackie Burke's makeup and he showed it now with thick, guttural confidence. "Just how in hell would I have found this camp if Jardene hadn't told me where to look? That straighten things out for you?"

"Maybe—maybe not," considered Fargo. "What's the word from Pinto?"

"You're to come to town with all your men. Right away."

"So! Why?"

"Near as I can gather, for a little visit to the C Cross headquarters—before mornin'."

Ned Fargo's cold and shadowed glance moved up and down Blackie Burke, weighing Burke's words, committing himself to nothing, probing for what might be truth and what might be lies.

Frank Allard touched Brack Harper's arm again, and the cattleman understood without words. There was just the faintest slither of sound as he inched backward. And presently Allard sensed, rather than heard, men of Harper's crew moving up to the vantage of the cut bank's crest. And then, a moment later, Allard had Harper again at his side.

Down by the fire, Blackie Burke brought out tobacco and papers and twisted up a smoke. There was a touch of calculated bravado in the act. There was also a certain shrewdness in Blackie Burke, for he hit right at the core of Ned Fargo's doubt.

"I know what you're thinkin', Fargo. The raid on the C Cross was to be pulled by Starke's outfit and that of Brack Harper. We're supposed to be the injured ones. In a way we are, and in another way we ain't." Burke paused to give out a short, harsh laugh. "Generally depends on how much money in your jeans you end up with that says how bad you're hurt. Well, the way this deal shapes up, we'll have money in our jeans. And a lot of it."

"Keep talkin'," said Ned Fargo.

Blackie Burke scratched a match and touched it to his cigarette. "Comin' up the trail our herd was raided. We lost a fair jag of cows, and one man. Well, trail hands come cheap and we figger to get our cattle back, plus a cut in the C Cross. It shapes up like this. Starke and Jardene ain't what you'd call completely satisfied with the stand that Brack Harper has taken. They're anything but sure he intends to go all the way with things. He's insisted on holding off hittin' the C Cross until tomorrow in daylight, which ain't what Starke and Jardene want. So they've made a deal just between themselves. They're going to hit the C Cross just before dawn. And so long as Harper and his outfit won't be there to help, Jardene wants you and your crowd to fill in. That's the way I get the picture, and Jardene will give you the other angles when you see him. He said not to waste any time, as night won't last forever."

Fargo's men, listening in surly, suspicious silence, now began to crowd the fire, arguing this thing.

"Ned," rapped one, "this fellow is lyin'!"

"How much dirty work we got to do?" put in another. "The C Cross ain't about to be sleepin' sound and stupid—not after that ruckus we met up with while pushin' stock onto the C Cross range earlier today. We go to ridin' our luck too wild we could bump into somethin' plenty rough."

Fargo waved them to silence, still studying Blackie Burke with a cold intentness. "The part I don't get is Pinto Jardene and Starke friending up so damn chummy," he growled. "Not unless Starke's turned complete damn fool. Past that, Pinto must have laid a lot of cards on the table."

"Which he probably has, and what I been tryin' to tell you," returned Burke easily. "Spread enough

190

money around and it can cover a lot of cards. Well, I've done what I was told to do—which was bring you Jardene's word. The rest is up to you."

Ned Fargo made a fast decision. "All right—we'll ride into town. But mister, you'll be ridin' with us. And if things ain't exactly as you claim, one other thing is damn certain. You'll never live to pick up any of that money off the table! Yeah, we'll ride."

At Frank Allard's shoulder, Brack Harper muttered, "It's now or never...!"

Frank Allard pushed up on one knee, drawing his gun while his voice rang across the night. "Wrong Fargo! You're not riding tonight. Don't anybody move!"

The stillness that followed might have been the shocked and breathless emptiness that could cover the world after some staggering and mind-boggling clap of thunder. But only for a moment. Then a man yelled in wild savagery.

"Knew it—knew he was lyin'! This is a trap. He tricked us, damn him!"

The blare of a gun smothered the rest. Blackie Burke reeled as the bullet took him. And even before he could fall, Ned Fargo struck with the merciless speed of a trapped wolf, and shot Burke twice more. Then Fargo turned his gun on the darkness of the cut bank.

Beside him, Frank Allard heard Brack Harper get a shot away. Then his own gun was bucking in recoil, again and again. Ned Fargo was lunging desperately for the shelter of the night beyond the reach of the fire, shooting as he went. He was at the very outer limit of that ruddy light, just another stride from the safety of deep shadow, when his lank figure jerked and tottered. He spun on his heels, throwing a final shot at the cut bank. Then he jackknifed at the waist and lunged out on his face.

All along the length of the cut bank now, guns were pounding. Another of Fargo's gang, trying for the shelter of darkness, never got there. He seemed to be diving headlong, but when he struck, he was loose and limp and lay as he landed, never moving.

Frank Allard went over the cut bank, sliding down in a welter of sod and gravel. "Their horses!" he yelled. "Don't let them get to their horses!"

Behind him, Brack Harper and his men came over the bank in a tumbling, sliding rush. Gaining his feet, Allard raced toward the upper end of the flat, where he'd heard those horses stamping. Guns were pounding out flat, rumbling reports from the blackness ahead, and as he ran on in, Allard crouched low, searching the dark for something definite to shoot at. But Brack Harper and his men, charging after him, were holding nothing back, answering the gunfire up ahead with more of the same.

A horse, stung by a stray bullet, snorted wildly and broke away at a wild run, and its fright caught up more of its kind. The tramp of hoofs broke into a furious, pounding rush. Clatter of gravel, crashing of brush, then the fading tumult of frantically running animals. A man cursed in wild, despairing anger. Up ahead the gunfire dwindled, frittered out.

Into the night, men were fleeing afoot, scattering, each intent now only on his own safety. Had they been able to gain their horses, they might have made a bitter fight of it, even though Ned Fargo, their leader, was down in a crumpled heap at the edge of the firelight. But it was another story when they were afoot. They had left only the night and its far blackness, and this they sought in disorganized panic. Surprise had been complete and merciless, and the whole thing over and done with in the brief measure of moments.

Frank Allard stopped, straightened, and called to Brack Harper. Answer came a few yards off to one side.

"Call in your men, Harper! Back to the fire!"

Allard went back along the flat to the beckoning light. He stopped at the fringe of it, marking with somber eyes the three figures sprawled there. Blackie

Burke had died at the guns of Fargo and his men. As for Fargo and that other one, both caught in the half-light, half-dark, who knew at what gun they had died? Maybe at his, thought Allard grimly, maybe at those of Brack Harper and his men. It had been so quick, so explosively sudden, and now it was over and here lay the bleak residue...

Men came straggling in, with Brack Harper in the lead. There was no exultancy, just the sudden weariness of a grim purpose fulfilled. One of them had a limply swinging arm in a shirt sleeve darkly soggy. Two of the other led him close to the fire and began bandaging the arm with faded neckerchiefs.

"How bad?" Allard asked.

"I'll live," was the gruff answer. "Missed the bone. Last damn shot they turned loose was what did it."

Brack Harper checked the wound and said, "There's a doctor in Pawnee, Joe. He'll fix you as good as new."

The cattleman came over to Allard. "You heard," he said bleakly. "Starke's turned renegade, too. I want to see that man. I want to look him in the eye and tell him off."

"And I," added Allard, "want to see Pinto Jardene. Better call in our horses."

At Harper's order a man went over to the cut bank and clawed a scrambling way up its steepness. Harper called after him. "You and Jenkins bring the horses in from lower down the creek. Trying to bring them down that bank in this dark could end up in some broken legs."

When Blackie Burke had been halted by Ned Fargo's challenge and then ordered to show himself at the fire, Burke had left his mount ground-reined some fifteen yards back in the outer dark. There the animal had stood quietly enough until the sudden eruption of gunfire had split the night wide open in rocketing violence. Spooked by this, the horse had reared and swung wide until, a good fifty yards away from the fire, the loose and dragging reins had tangled in an old driftwood snag, forming a tie strong enough to hold the horse even through the tumult of stampede higher up the flat. Now, in that shocked stillness which held as an aftermath of battle, the animal stood fairly quiet once again.

The soft and smooth murmur of a man's voice reached its pricked and enquiring ears, and the horse relaxed still more, for this it understood and was comforted by. The man low-crouched, cautious in his stealing approach. He got a hand on the reins, straightened up by the horse's sheltering bulk, ran another hand back and forth along the neck of the animal. He freed the tangled reins, turned the horse. Then in one leap he was in the saddle, using his spurs deep and cruelly, and the horse, under this punishment, surged into full stride and raced away.

This sudden rush of hoofs brought the group about the fire up in a fresh alertness. It was Frank Allard who first understood. He yelled harshly.

"Burke's horse, of course! One of Fargo's crowd remembered while we forgot. And he could be heading for town!"

All sound of that speeding horse had faded out by the time their own mounts were brought up. Then they too hit their saddles, raced across the island flat, crashed through the creek growth on the far side, and headed away to the east toward Pawnee, where certain men would be sitting and elaborating on their predatory schemes.

Back on the island flat in Plume Creek, the fire once again began to dwindle, while the deep dark crept in to roll over and hide the night's scars.

Men held their racing mounts to it without letup, and as a group began to string out, the stronger horses moving ahead, the weaker ones dropping slowly back. Frank Allard and Brack Harper held pace with the leaders. They passed no words back and forth, as there was no need of these. Both realized full well that this night was not yet done, nor were things finished that had to be finished. For this sort of an affair was not something that could be started, then left hanging unfinished, only partly done. To this a full answer had to be written, one way or another.

Much depended on the destination of the rustler who had made off on Black Burke's horse. If the fellow was merely fleeing toward personal sanctuary somewhere, then there was no need of this hard, punishing race of pursuit. On the other hand, however, if the man was heading for town, to report the night's happenings to Pinto Jardene, then the trail was far from being run down. Of only one thing could they be sure, which was that the fellow had gained a good start on them. So they had to hold their straining mounts to it and drive them hard.

Night's blackness became a taunting emptiness, with a depth that constantly challenged them, but which they could never quite reach. It was a black wall that gave way before them and rushed past them on either side. The pound of hoofs was a steady rumble that clung close to the earth and flowed away behind them. The rawly acrid scent of sweating horseflesh lifted warm and penetrating and seemed to close out the fresh, keen breath of the night.

Even the stronger running mounts were beginning to labor and falter a little in their stride by the time they picked up the late-lingering lights of Pawnee out ahead. And now, against the glow of those lights, they caught a glimpse of the bobbing head and shoulders of a speeding rider.

"Afraid of that!" Allard called. "He's out to warn Jardene. We got to get in there, Brack!"

Now it was spurs and quirts together, wringing a last burst of effort from near run-out horses. Abruptly the town lifted and bulked and then they were pounding into the west end of the street and tearing straight on for the Palace. They saw the rider ahead, caught clear now in the reflected, garish glow of the Palace's lights, leave his saddle at a leap, dart up and across the porch and on inside.

Frank Allard left his own saddle while his horse was still in near full stride, skidded, staggered, dug in his heels, then caught his balance, and was at the door of the Palace in two long leaps. Brack Harper was right behind him, and Harper's men a ragged tide of running men pounding at Harper's heels.

For this hour of the night the big barroom of the Palace was fairly crowded. Many of those present were Slash S riders, and when Frank Allard lunged through the door of the place there was a concerted shift of these men which bunched them, hard-faced, alert, and wary. Leaning against the bar, smoking a cigar, was Lee Mosby, and when he saw Allard he gave out a startled exclamation.

"Frank! What the hell—"

"You'll know later, Lee," shot back Allard. "Right now, keep the top on this room. Gun the first man who tries to start anything. Harper, tell your men to back Mosby's hand if he needs help!"

Allard drove straight for the door of the back room with Brack Harper rapping a curt order to his crew as he pushed at Allard's heels.

There was a key grating in the lock of the door of the room as Allard reached it. Drawing his gun he threw his full weight against the door, and the lock, just beginning to turn, did not have purchase enough to hold against Allard's smashing drive. The door crashed back, forcing a cursing figure ahead of it, the figure of Pinto Jardene. Then Allard was through, the muzzle of his gun sweeping the room in a ready arc of threat. His words, coldly dominant, were an equal threat.

"Watch yourselves—everybody! This is for keeps!"

Only two others besides Jardene were in the room.

Abel Starke for one, the other the member of Ned Fargo's rustler band who, held by some blind twist of loyalty to Jardene, had made this desperate race to carry warning to Jardene, and lost it by the space of short minutes. He stood now by that center table, panting as though he had done the running, not his horse. Ragged hair hung down across his forehead and his half-open lips were pulled into a desperate snarl. Allard's gun settled in line with him.

"Don't try it!" warned Allard. "Put your gun on that table and back away—to that far wall. Careful now!" The lock of Allard's gun clicked. "I don't want to have to kill you!"

The rustler was held in indecision for a few ticking seconds, then shrugged resignedly, lifted his gun from the holster with thumb and forefinger, put the weapon on the table, and backed away to the designated wall. He'd done his best in this thing. Now let somebody else play the hand from here.

The moment the unpredictable threat of the rustler was removed, Allard put his full attention on Pinto Jardene, while Brack Harper now moved past Allard and over to face Abel Starke.

Starke, who had evidently been sitting at the table when the rustler had burst into the room, now was on his feet, bracing himself with the back of his chair. In the tight pull of his features and the settled glare of his eyes, there was reflected a great and sudden fear, but also something that was plainly venomous. He flinched visibly at the first lash of Brack Harper's words.

"All right, Starke—now I know. Once I had you figured as being at least half a man. I was wrong. You're nothing but a slippery, crooked rat, posing as being an honest man. Instead you're a cheap, would-be thief. I wish you had the guts to make a try for a gun, but I'm afraid you won't. How about it?"

Abel Starke ran the tip of his tongue across pinched, fear-parched lips. His voice was a dry croak.

"I don't understand you, Harper—don't understand you at all. What's the war talk about? What you driving at?"

Now it was Pinto Jardene who spoke. "I'd like a little information myself. Allard, you better have a damned good reason for this kind of high-handed business."

The dive owner had steadied from the smashing impact of the door slamming open in his face. He had instinctively smoothed his rumpled clothes, and now he stood, sleek-faced and dark, almost imperturbable except for the hard shining of his black eyes. Looking at him, Frank Allard thought that, if nothing else, Pinto Jardene was a master gambler.

"I've a reason, Jardene," Allard told him. "Good enough for me. First, chew on these facts. Ned Fargo is dead. So is Blackie Burke. There will be no move against the C Cross tonight, tomorrow, or at any other time. You rigged a pretty ambitious hand, and you were set to play it strong, for a big pot. But this is a showdown, and you don't hold enough cards."

Pinto Jardene's expression did not change. "I don't know what you're talking about."

Allard waved his free hand in a weary gesture. "I said this was a showdown, Jardene. I've looked at all your cards; now you're looking at mine. And a bluff is good only to the point where the cards are turned face up. They're that way, now. You lose, Jardene!"

The legs of Abel Starke's chair grated as he pushed against it. "I'm getting out of here," he said thinly. "Jardene, what's between you and this fellow Allard, is all your affair. Yeah, I'm getting out of here."

Jardene did not answer, but when his glance touched Starke, it went up and down him in scathing contempt. Starke started to move away from the table, but Brack Harper caught him by the shoulder, whirled him, and slammed him into his chair.

"You're staying put," Harper growled. "Maybe from the point of actual action you're clear, but by intent you're a low, greedy crook. You heard Allard tell that your rider, Blackie Burke is dead. And he is—plenty! But before he got it, Allard and I heard everything he had to tell that Fargo *hombre*. We listened in on every word. A little deal, was the way Burke put it—a deal just between Jardene and you. A smash raid on this C Cross outfit, just before dawn. And then a good spread of money for all the faithful. Starke, when you tie in with a flock of thieves, then you're one of them!"

Harper swung his glance to Pinto Jardene. "Just want you to know, Jardene, that smooth as your story was, it didn't get over all the way with me. I'm not that big a sucker. Oh, I was going to ride out to the C Cross with Starke tomorrow. But I was damn sure about one angle. Which was that there would be no showdown with the C Cross unless I'd found a lot more proof of a raid against my herd than what you'd shown me. I was going to get the C Cross's side of the story before I started any trouble—or allowed it to start, for that matter. I think you realized that right from the first, which was the main reason why you cooked up this deal with Starke."

Listening and watching closely, Frank Allard saw a faint tide of darkening color seep across Pinto Jardene's smooth face, while the hard, metallic glitter in Jardene's eyes deepened. Then Allard gave a final twist of the knife.

"Haley Twitchell didn't prove out a very stout prop to lean on, did he?"

Jardene's lips thinned with sudden pressure. "Twitchell's just a gutless, slobbering fool! All right, Allard—say you've guessed right. Say you've spoiled a good game for me. For my cards weren't high enough. That's still as much harm as you can do me. You'd have a hell of a time proving enough before a jury to tie me down. So now, suppose you get the hell out of here!"

Allard's gray eyes bored into the dive owner's black ones. "So you'd try another bluff, eh Jardene?" he said dryly. "Well, it's still no good, and it won't work. Ned Fargo and his gang might have done the actual rustling, but you gave the orders—you were the real head of the thing. And you don't slide out from under. You face the music, and it's a rough tune. Brack Harper here says there's only one real cure for a cow thief— and I agree with him. Brack's herd was one that you hit, which makes him the injured party. So I'm turning you over to Brack and his men. Suit you, Brack?"

"Right down the line," answered Harper ominously. "Me and my boys will set up a lesson and a cure that'll benefit all the other herds coming up the trail. I'd like to cut two ropes, one for Starke here...But he just does manage to wiggle free of that. Yet he'll pay, too. I'll see that the word goes out, up and down the trail. I'll see that it reaches his home range as well, and it will brand him for the rest of his days. No honest man will look at him. Out in that other room he's got some good boys, whom he misled in this mess. When they know the real truth, they'll spit in his face. So I don't think Mister Abel Starke is set to enjoy the future, either. Sound all right to you, Frank?"

"Just about."

"Then," growled Harper, "let's get this thing finished. Jardene, you're going on a ride with me and my men!"

While Brack Harper had been speaking, Pinto Jardene brought a cigar from a vest pocket and was rolling it across his lips. Now he was reaching into a lower vest pocket for a match. But suddenly the flush across his dark face became burning spots of hard crimson, and his words were a softly desperate purr.

"No ride, Harper—not now or ever!"

Then it wasn't a match he brought from his vest pocket. It was a stubby, twin-barreled, nickel-plated derringer. A vest-pocket gun, a deadly across-the-table gun. A gambler's gun. And to the last, Pinto Jardene was a gambler....

It might have paid off, this last bitter gamble. It would have paid off if Brack Harper had been alone. For Harper had put his gun back in the leather and, no matter how fast his draw, he'd have been behind Jardene.

Even Frank Allard might have been slow, for Jardene's flashing move, in the face of all odds, was a step of desperation few men would have attempted. But as Jardene's hand whipped from his pocket, there was that gleam of nickeled gun metal in the lamplight...

So then Frank Allard made the only move he could have. The draw he made and the shot he threw was instinctive, rather than calculated. The smash of recoil drove Allard's arm back, and at this range there could be no missing. A convulsive ripple of movement ran through Pinto Jardene. Then, even while the room still shuddered under the rumble of report, the dive owner wilted limply down. The derringer, falling from his hand, made a small clatter of sound against the floor.

A short silence fell, broken finally by a gusty, hard breath breaking from the lips of the rustler standing against the far wall. Harper, his gun now drawn, whirled to watch the fellow, but the rustler made no move. His part in this thing had been played out long before. While Abel Starke sank lower and lower in his chair, seeming to shrivel, his face gray with a great and sudden fear.

Then it was Lee Mosby's big shout, coming in from the outer room.

"Frank—Frank Allard!"

Rushing in, Mosby came to an abrupt stop, exclaiming with lowered voice at sight of Pinto Jardene's crumpled figure.

"God's name, Frank! What...?"

"He drew for an ace, Lee," informed Allard tonelessly. "And it came up—black!"

CHAPTER THIRTEEN

SEATED IN his office chair, Haley Twitchell was a gross bulk. His shoulders sagged until there seemed to be no points to them at all and his body was a slope flowing down from his neck to meet with the up-pushing bulge of his paunch. He was as formless as a crumpled toad, and with no more fiber. His heavy lips sagged half-open, and for once the inevitable cigar was missing.

In another chair Royce, the son, sat, more erect than his sire and, while there was a banked hate in his eyes, there was no spark of courage behind it to give vitality or meaning to that hate. It was a blank, ugly thing, but there would never be any danger in it.

Standing with his back to the window and looming

a rangy, solid figure against the morning sunshine outside, Frank Allard read young Royce's hate and dismissed it as meaningless. All the while his own glance bored coldly at the crumpled banker beyond the desk.

Allard had been speaking, his words level and measured. Now he paused to build and light a cigarette before finishing.

"So there all of it is, Twitchell. Some of us know your part in the big scheme of thievery and loot. In the eyes of those who know, you're not one damned bit better than was Pinto Jardene. Not as good, for that matter, for he had the nerve to see it through, regardless. The stickler is, this town and the country around it, such as the Bench, had no need for Jardene. But it has need for you, because of your bank. For that reason alone, you're going to stay here.

"We who know your true colors will keep our mouths shut, so long as you run your business straight up and down and don't get any more ambitious and crooked ideas. But if you slip over the line just once, then God help you, for mere humans won't. They'll hang you high as hell! I guess that's all."

Allard turned and went out. He had to get outside. He had to get clean air in his lungs and the feel of the bright, good sunshine on his face. Also, he had to gear himself up to one final chore, the doing of which would surely lay a black and forbidding scar across his soul.

He strode slowly toward the hotel, a tall man who threw a long shadow. In the sun's bright pour, the town lay almost drowsy, the street empty. Over at the Palace the doors were locked and all was silence. Farther west along the street the dives and deadfalls were quiet, and in them men were wondering about heading out of this town and seeking another nearer to their liking and more tolerant of their kind of trade. For just now the shadow of one man lay full and strong across this town of Pawnee—the shadow of Frank Allard.

A brown-faced cowboy came around the corner of the hotel, sober and troubled. Allard stopped and spoke.

"Hello, Sam. Made that deal yet with Con Waters for that horse?"

Sam Lorry nodded. "Got everything, Mister Allard—except Nell. Paxton won't let her out of his sight. There's something queer about that man. He scares me."

Allard spun his cigarette butt aside. "Have a little patience, Sam. You and Nell are young. By tomorrow you and Nell will be free to ride. You'll see. How about the rest of the Slash S punchers? What are they going to do now?"

"They've thrown their camp in with Brack Harper's layout," said Sam. "Going back down the trail together. Understand that Harper's figuring on pulling out tomorrow morning. But Starke," and here Sam paused and spat in contempt, "he musta cut and run by himself. Anyway, he's gone—the mangy crook! Makes me ashamed to think I once rode for him and took his pay. What makes a man turn coyote like he did?"

Allard dropped a hand on Sam Lorry's muscular young shoulder. "There's no good answer to some humans, Sam. I'll be seeing you later."

He turned in at the hotel and climbed to his room. Morning's sun had already sifted a pleasant warmth into the place. He pulled the chair up to the window and sat there, looking out across town and the beckoning sweep of country beyond. He had come to this town primarily to gather a certain knowledge. And now he possessed that knowledge, and it lay bitter and mocking across his mind.

There was a step in the hall and a knock at the door. It was Con Waters who entered at Allard's gruff summons. Con closed the door carefully, then stood with his back to it, studying Allard with grave, troubled eyes. "I'll want a bit of your time, Frank."

"Got plenty of it, Con," Allard said. "Help yourself."

Con came over and sat on the edge of the bed. "So you've brought it fully to heel," murmured Con. "The town, I mean. And you no longer wear your badge, which means you probably have other ideas and new purposes. Of these I am curious."

He's shrewd, thought Allard. As shrewd a man as any I ever knew. He knows what's in my mind and there's no use trying to hide it from him.

Aloud, Allard said, "Con, I know who killed Jim Creightly. And you know who did it, too."

Con became very still. When he answered there was strain in his voice. "What makes you so sure, man?"

Allard touched his head and his heart. "In here, somehow. For he hasn't told the truth of the thing, and there is no one he could be covering up for but himself. Yes, Con—I'm sure."

Con sighed deeply. "From the first I had the feeling that you would someday know. Yes, Frank—Gil Paxton killed Jim Creightly. The answer has come to me the same way it has to you, by head and heart and because there is no other answer that made sense. And so, now that you know, what are your intentions?"

Harshness surged up in Allard, roughening his words. "I came to Pawnee to kill the man who gunned my partner!"

Con's head lifted and his glance was bitterly straight. "That, Frank, you cannot do."

The harshness in Allard deepened. "Name me one good reason why I can't."

"I can give you a dozen," said Con stoutly. "We'll get at them, one at a time."

Allard was silent, studying this gaunt and purposeful man.

"The first reason," went on Con, "is because you are the man you are. There is a streak of iron in your makeup, but there is also a fine appreciation for life and a good, smiling world. Also, there is a fundamental kindness in you that you would sometimes hide, yet is always there for any man to see should he look closely enough. And that kindness will not let you hurt people who do not deserve to be hurt."

"What about Jim Creightly?" growled Allard. "He's dead, yes, and maybe his pain was short. But I've his memory to live with. What about that, Con?"

"A man is dead," said Con slowly. "He did not deserve to die—yet he is dead. He is dead because he knew a misunderstood kindness and sympathy for a lonely girl. But Jim Creightly would be the last man in the world to have that girl hurt again."

Allard got up, took a turn back and forth across the room. "You're referring to Nell Kane, of course?"

"I'm thinking of Nell Kane for one," Con nodded. "Fourteen years old she was, when a lynch rope took her own father away. Since then, for better or worse, Gil Paxton has been her second father. Oh, I know she's resented the life Paxton has held her to, blind to the yearnings of a girl who has become a woman. Yet he has given her a home, he's sheltered her and fed her and given her a certain security. And while there are times when the girl has surely hated him, yet I know that deep inside her he has claimed some small part of her affections. It could not be otherwise."

"And why," demanded Allard savagely, "has he done these things for her? Because there is a damned crazy, dark twist in the man that's made him feel he must possess a woman in name, if no other way. He lost his wife to another man and he would replace her image in Nell, and deny the girl her rightful gifts of life, just to feed his black, locoed obsession. He killed a good man because of that obsession. I say Gil Paxton deserves nothing!"

Con Waters seemed not to have heard Allard's harsh statement as he went on, quiet and imperturbable. "Then there is another. I can remember her when she was just a little twig of a lass, with her fair hair in pigtails, in child-size boots, and bib overalls. She would come riding into town with her father in a spring wagon, and while her father would dicker with Gil Paxton for ranch supplies, she would scamper about the store, playing imaginary childish games. And always, before she left, Gil Paxton would tuck a bit of hard candy in her hand and send her away full of childish glee."

Con got out a blackened and beloved pipe, tamped fine cut tobacco into it with a calloused forefinger, then passed a flaming match back and forth across the bowl, his gaunt cheeks caving inward as he puffed.

"That little girl is a young woman, now," he went on. "And a glorious one. You have done some fine things for her and for her ranch in these past few hours, things she will hear about. And what she will hear will make you a big man in her eyes, a very big man. It is a fine thing to be a big and great man in the eyes of such as Barbara Chancellor—aye, a fine thing. But should you kill Gil Paxton, then what would she think of you, even though she heard the truth as to why you killed him? This man she has known and dealt with all her life, and whom she thinks of as a kind and generous old friend? I know what she would think and how she would feel. She would no longer see you as she does now. Instead she would see you as something that had laid a dark and frightening shadow across all her memories. How big a price do you want to pay, Frank Allard, just to satisfy a feeling of personal vengeance?"

Allard paced the room again. "Damn you, Con!" he burst out. "You take a man all apart!"

"There is one more thing," said Con. "You pinned on a badge of law. You polished that badge and you wore it with a cool, good pride. That badge meant something with you behind it. You lifted another man with a badge back to his feet, when he had all but forgotten his pride and integrity. And should you kill Gil Paxton now, then you would wipe out what you've given to Lee Mosby, and leave him forever more a man who will not believe

208

in anything, not even himself. Frank, you can't do it. When you think of all these things—you can't do it."

Allard stopped at the window, staring out, his back to Con Waters, who studied that tall, rangy figure and those square and solid shoulders.

"A last word," said Con. "The man himself—Gil Paxton. I am not condoning his act, understand. It is a black chapter he must live with all his life and so be a great punishment. Still, strange as it may seem, there is good in the man. There is a certain uncompromising honesty in him. He held that money in trust for you, every last cent of it. I have known him long, and I have seen much of that honesty before. Nor is the man niggardly. I have seen him stock the wagons of down and out nester families and take no money in return. Particularly when there were big-eyed, solemn, hungry children in those wagons. I say there is much good in the man. That in one way he has lacked balance is his own great misfortune and punishment. We who do not suffer any dark twists in our natures find it hard to understand and make allowances. Yet we would be small men if we did not try."

Silence fell, and the gurgle of Con's old pipe was the only small sound across the room. Abruptly Frank Allard whirled, came around the end of the bed, and held out his hand.

"Thanks, Con," he said gruffly. "Thanks for keeping me sane. I'll not kill Gil Paxton. I'm going to have a talk with him, but I'll not kill him. And Con—I hope you live a thousand years, for a sometimes crazy and mixed-up world could use you as a balance."

It was a big, warm smile that lit up Con's gaunt and homely face as their hands met. His eyes shone and a bit of ancient brogue touched his tongue richly. "'Tis a fine and understanding friendship we'll know, Frank Allard—you and I."

* * *

The store, like the street outside, was empty. Except for Gil Paxton. The storekeeper was fussing about, absently doing all the little things that had become sheer habit with him down across the years, at times like this when trade was slack and the store empty of all except silence: straightening an item on a shelf here, tucking in some loose end there. He turned to the sound of Frank Allard's step.

The past few days had wrought a change in Gil Paxton. He seemed thinned down, and there were drawn lines of tension and a sort of bewildered complexity in his face. He had the look of a man being pushed one way by one force, and pulled in an opposite way by another. He gave Allard a short nod, then stood waiting, silent.

Allard perched sideways on the counter, at ease, yet with a certain alertness. "I'll take that money now," he said quietly. "Need it for a deal. I'm buying the old Kane place from Nell. All right with you, of course?"

A certain stiffness ran through Gil Paxton. That same stiffness was in his answer, making his words dry and spaced and a little jerky. "News to me—that Nell wants to sell. Why—should she?"

"Nell's leaving," Allard told him. "Tomorrow morning. With the man she's going to marry, Sam Lorry. They'll make a fine pair and find all the happiness the ups and downs of life allow any pair of mortals. So, while the old home place would be of no further good to Nell, the money for it would. Young folks, starting out in life, can always use a little nest egg, and I can use the range. So, we're going to make that deal."

"Maybe," said Paxton in that same stiff way. "Maybe you're taking a lot for granted, Allard. Maybe I got something to say about all this."

"Sure you have," drawled Allard. "You're going to put your approval on everything. You're going to agree to everything that will be best for Nell and Sam, and you're going to send them away without any doubts or dark memories. You're going to shake Sam's hand because it is a good and reliable hand. That's what you're going to do."

Their eyes met and held. "You're very sure of yourself, aren't you, Allard?" said Gil Paxton, his voice flat and toneless.

Allard jerked a curt nod. "Very. For you see, Paxton—I know you weren't in this store the night Jim Creightly was killed. You've told me you were—but you weren't. And you didn't hear anybody running down-street, after the shot, because nobody did run down it. I know these things and so do other men in this town who are more generous than you've ever been in your life. They've been liberal in their judgment of you because they know the things that have happened in your life—things that could twist any man's perspective. For that reason they have made allowances, and given you the benefit of the doubt. Now I'm trying to make those allowances. And it is hard for me to do so, for Jim Creightly was my partner. But I'm trying. Don't make it too hard for me."

Gil Paxton's normally somewhat ruddy face had drained to an ash-gray. He stared at Allard out of eyes gone suddenly hopeless and haggard. His lips moved woodenly. "So—you know?"

"That you killed Jim Creightly? Yes, I know." Allard slid off the counter and loomed over Paxton in swift harshness. "Why did you do it—why did you kill that man? Did you have any legitimate reason that can make this thing any easier for me to take? Speak up, man—did you?"

Gil Paxton seemed to shrink all over, and his glance faltered and went away under Allard's bleak stare. For a moment he seemed unable to find words. Then he spoke slowly and with a great weariness.

"Yes, I felt I had a reason. At the time it made sense to me. But as I've thought about it since—and God knows I've done my share of thinking about it—I know

I really had no good reason and that what I did was, in effect, murder. Since then I've lived with that knowledge, night and day. And if ever any man has crawled back and forth through the fires of hell, I am that man!"

Paxton's voice frittered out, and Allard remained silent, knowing there was more to come. Paxton sighed deeply.

"I'm not asking for sympathy, for I deserve none. It—it all began when—when my wife ran away with another man. No doubt I was to blame for that, too—for I was blind to so many things she craved and had a right to. But—but the happening did things to me. Inside. In my heart and head. I guess you might say I lost some kind of fundamental sense of balance. I craved companionship and affection with one hand, yet with the other I held it away from me. I took in a fourteen-year-old orphan girl, Nell, and gave her a home. I intended to play the part of a good father to her, but it seems I've made a sorry mess of that, too."

Paxton paused for a moment, as though marshalling and weighing his thoughts. Then he cleared his throat and went on.

"I failed in that because I refused her the companionship a young girl naturally yearns for. Because I distrusted men—all of them. When I saw a man of near her own age talking to Nell, a sort of black craziness rose up in me. I drove them away, and in doing so, I guess I drove Nell away from me, too. So it went, until Jim Creightly came along. I saw that Nell liked him, for he had a gay and happy way about him. I can see now that he meant no ill by the girl at all. But at that time the black craziness had me by the throat. I had words with him about it, telling him to stay away from Nell. He laughed at me and told me I was a locoed old fool. He was right.

"But that didn't change the dark mood at the time. I brooded and brooded over it. In my twisted thinking all soundedness of understanding left me and the conviction came over me that I'd have to kill Jim Creightly to protect Nell. I knew that Creightly was in the habit of coming down to Con Waters' stable every evening to brush and curry and take care of his horse, of which he was very fond. So, that black and crazy night I laid for him, fully intending to shoot him in the back."

Paxton paused again, swinging his head from side to side while rubbing a hand back and forth across his forehead and eyes. "I—I was crazy—I must have been. But I laid for him. He came down the street, whistling in the soft, cheery way he had. And when he had passed me, I came up behind him. And then—you can believe me or not, though I swear it is the truth—I found I couldn't pull the trigger—not deliberately. At that moment Creightly seemed to sense someone behind him for he whirled and leaped at me. In the deep darkness we fought, he to get the gun away from me. I to get clear away from this foul thing I'd been contemplating. I—I can't recall exactly what happened in those few wild moments, out in that black street. We were twisting and turning and wrestling...Then the gun went off and Jim Creightly groaned and went down."

Gil Paxton sagged back against the counter, his shaking hands across his face. Presently he straightened slowly and his hands dropped to his sides. His head lifted and he looked fairly at Frank Allard, out of those haggard, beaten eyes.

"So there it is," he said simply. "That was what happened and how it happened. That—is the truth. It seems I've come finally to the truth, and I feel the better for it. But that night I lied. I lied to many people, but I couldn't lie to myself. I even lied to the man I killed, and that is as black a lie as any man ever uttered. In the thick darkness he couldn't tell who it was he was struggling with, who had shot him, and I didn't tell him, because I was afraid. But I'm afraid no longer. You came to this town, Frank Allard, to avenge your partner. You're looking at the man who killed him. Now you can kill me. I've got it coming."

For a long, long moment Frank Allard stood motionless, with carven, expressionless features, his eyes blank with the dust of old memories. Finally he shook himself and spoke softly, almost as if his words were inner thoughts coming aloud.

"Yes, I could kill you. And walk out of this town a free man when the word got out as to why I did it. But that wouldn't prove anything and it wouldn't cure anything. It would only hurt people who do not deserve to be hurt. Those are Con Waters' words. A great man, Con Waters."

He looked at Paxton out of somber, shadowed eyes. "I ought to hate you, but I can't. Maybe I pity you. I don't know. But I do know this. You got something to live with all your days, and you'll find them long days. Yet you have a final chance to know some sort of peace. There is a small glint of happiness right before you, Paxton. Don't pass it up for the chance will never come to you again! Now I'll take that money, and I'll be back later to close the deal with Nell."

Paxton went slowly over to his safe and came back with the weighty canvas sack. He looked briefly into Allard's eyes again, then spoke one husky word.

"Thanks!"

When Allard went out, Gil Paxton leaned against the counter for long, long moments, his head bowed, his face working. Then he straightened up, cleared his throat, and sent a call echoing up the stairway.

"Nell! Would you come down here, please?"

She came slowly, a little uncertainly. She stood before him and said, "What did you want?" Then, as she fully saw the expression on Paxton's face, she caught her breath.

"I'm afraid, Nell," said Paxton slowly, "that I haven't been all I should to you. As a foster father I've been a pretty poor mistake. I'm sorry about that, and would try and make it up to you. Tell me—you love Sam Lorry? You want to go away with him?"

She twisted her hands, hardly able to believe this sudden gentleness she saw in Paxton's eyes.

"Yes," she said. "Yes, I do." Then she added, with sudden, deep intuitiveness, "I'll remember you always, Mister Paxton. For I think you've tried to be good to me...."

"Not nearly as good as I should have been, Nell. But I'm going to make up for all that now. Tomorrow morning you and Sam can leave and we'll make it a fine, good occasion. You'll have all the world before you, and it will be a fine, great world if you and Sam work together to make it so. Now we're going to be busy the rest of the day, child—getting a real outfit together for you—getting everything squared away. And I think we should celebrate. So you run along and find Sam and tell him he's to come to supper, for the three of us will want to talk."

She stared at him, her eyes wide and misting. "You—you really mean all this, do you? You really are going to give Sam and me your blessing?"

"Yes, Nell—all of that. And if you'll just write to me regular, so I'll know how things are going with you—"

Before he could say more, strong young arms were hugging Gil Paxton, and tears and lips were warm on his cheek. And the girl was sobbing her great happiness.

"Oh, I wanted this—I wanted this! It makes everything so right—so right...!"

CHAPTER FOURTEEN

SO NOW it was one more morning and there was considerable activity in front of Gil Paxton's store. A spring wagon was there. Not a new wagon, but a good sound one that had done some duty in the past out of Con Waters' livery establishment. The back of it was piled high with a great many things, all covered with a heavy tarp and tied down snugly with rope lashings. A stout team was harnessed to the rig, and a pair of saddle broncs were tied at lead behind.

Con Waters was there, and Ben Ripon. So was Lee Mosby and Frank Allard. Gil Paxton came out of the store, one arm around Nell Kane, the other around Sam Lorry. Sam was all one great, shining grin. He wrung Gil Paxton's hand again and again, before dropping down off the porch and untying the halter ropes of the spring wagon team.

Nell Kane gave Gil Paxton a final hug and the same to gaunt old Con Waters. She shook hands with Lee Mosby and Ben Ripon and colored warmly under their gentle smiles and teasing words. Then she stood in front of Frank Allard, her eyes misty, her lips tremulous. She was too full of emotion to speak, but Allard understood.

"I'm sure Sam won't mind, Nell," he said softly. He bent his head and kissed her.

Then there was Sam, to shake his hand. Allard grinned and said, "I'm betting on you, Sam. Don't make me a loser."

"You can spend that bet money right now," vowed Sam stoutly. "It's that safe."

Allard's grip was iron. "I'm sure of that, boy. Good luck!"

Then Sam and Nell were up on the spring wagon seat, the wheels began to turn, and the rig rolled away, out of the east end of the street and then south, with the world all bright and beckoning distance.

Ben Ripon touched Allard's arm. "There's a lady waiting at the hotel for you, Frank. Said she'd like to speak to you when you had time."

Allard turned and looked along the street. She was standing on the hotel porch, a slim, straight figure. Allard knew a stir of quickening emotion as he headed quietly back there, touching his hat as he climbed the low stairs.

"Good morning, Barbara. How's my friend Lafe Oglevie making out?"

"Almost too good, and cranky as sin," was her answer. "Wanting to see you, as there is so much he wants to ask you about. That seemed quite an occasion over at the store. What was it all about?"

Allard smiled warmly. "A pair of fine young folks, Sam Lorry and Nell Kane, starting out on the trail of life together. They carry the best wishes of a lot of good people with them."

"I would like to add mine, along with the hope that they will be very happy," Barbara Chancellor said, speaking with convincing sincerity. She was soberly grave, a mood which became her, bringing as it did a settled sweetness to her face. Then, as Allard watched her silently, she added, "What's now for you, Frank? Ben Ripon has told me all you have done, which has to put this town and the C Cross ranch and its people, forever in your debt. Yet, that part is past. What is the future?"

"To stay put," he told her simply. "And I'm afraid you're not going to like this, Barbara. Because it's about the old Kane place. I've bougnt it, and I know you've wanted it yourself. But it is the one spot I've been looking for all my life, seems like."

"Why then, I'm glad you have it," Barbara approved quietly. "While hoping it will always remain what you've wished for."

His smile was small, musing, a little twisted. "Lot of hard work ahead, but that's all right, too. Hanging around town makes a man soft, but up there on the Bench...! I understand there's around a hundred head of Durham cattle rustled from Brack Harper, now running on your range. I made a deal with Harper for those cattle to stock my own place. Soon as I can, I'll get them off your grass and onto my own. There's also about the same number of Slash S stuff running loose. They'll have to be cut out and sold some where and the money sent south to Harper, who'll see that it gets to Abel Starke. That fellow Starke doesn't deserve such fair treatment, but it will serve to emphasize his own crookedness, a fact he'll have to live with for the rest of his days. When that's all cleaned up, then I'll settle down as a neighbor of yours."

Barbara nodded slowly. "All just prosaic business, is that it?"

"That," murmured Allard, "could depend."

She met his glance and held it, while quickening color stole into her cheeks and her eyes went suddenly very deep and luminously soft. And then it all lay, clear and fine and with a complete understanding in the hearts and minds and consciousness of both of them. Allard reached out and took her hand and she made no effort to withdraw it.

"Right now, my dear," he said. "I'm completely fed up with this town. That Bench up there is better country. Our kind of country."

Her slim fingers tightened around his and her voice ran very soft. "Just so! Good country. Our kind of country."

ABOUT THE AUTHOR

L.P. Holmes, born in a snowed-in log cabin in a Rockie Mountain gold camp, spent his early childhood in California's Mother Lode country. From there, his family went into the cattle business and moved to Napa Valley, where L.P. Holmes grew up, surrounded by horses, cattle, and the life of the ranch.

All his life, L.P. Holmes has had the itch to write. PAYOFF AT PAWNEE is his fifty-first novel. In addition to over six hundred short stories and novelettes, he has written articles on guns, hunting, and shooting.

L.P. Holmes still lives in Napa Valley. His hobbies haven't changed either from the ones he had as a kid: shooting guns, living the life outdoors, and, of course, writing books.

Renegade by Ramsay Thorne

___#1		(C30-827, $2.25)
___#2	BLOOD RUNNER	(C30-780, $2.25)
___#3	FEAR MERCHANT	(C30-774, $2.25)
___#4	DEATH HUNTER	(C90-902, $1.95)
___#5	MUCUMBA KILLER	(C30-775, $2.25)
___#6	PANAMA GUNNER	(C30-829, $2.25)
___#8	OVER THE ANDES TO HELL	(C30-781, $2.25)
___#9	HELL RAIDER	(C30-777, $2.25)
___#10	THE GREAT GAME	(C30-830, $2.25)
___#11	CITADEL OF DEATH	(C30-778, $2.25)
___#12	THE BADLANDS BRIGADE	(C30-779, $2.25)
___#13	THE MAHOGANY PIRATES	(C30-123, $1.95)
___#14	HARVEST OF DEATH	(C30-124, $1.95)
___#16	MEXICAN MARAUDER	(C32-253, $2.50)
___#17	SLAUGHTER IN SINALOA	(C30-257, $2.25)
___#18	CAVERN OF DOOM	(C30-258, $2.25)
___#19	HELLFIRE IN HONDURAS	(C30-630, $2.25, U.S.A.)
		(C30-818, $2.95, CAN.)
___#20	SHOTS AT SUNRISE	(C30-631, $2.25, U.S.A.)
		(C30-878, $2.95, CAN.)
___#21	RIVER OF REVENGE	(C30-632, $2.50, U.S.A.)
		(C30-963, $3.25, CAN.)
___#22	PAYOFF IN PANAMA	(C30-984, $2.50, U.S.A.)
		(C30-985, $3.25, CAN.)
___#23	VOLCANO OF VIOLENCE	(C30-986, $2.50, U.S.A.)
		(C30-987, $3.25, CAN.)
___#24	GUATEMALA GUNMAN	(C30-988, $2.50, U.S.A.)
		(C30-989, $3.25, CAN.)
___#25	HIGH SEA SHOWDOWN	(C30-990, $2.50, U.S.A.)
		(C30-991, $3.25, CAN.)
___#26	BLOOD ON THE BORDER	(C30-992, $2.50, U.S.A.)
		(C30-993, $3.25, CAN.)
___#27	SAVAGE SAFARI	(C30-995, $2.50, U.S.A.)
		(C30-994, $3.25, CAN.)

WARNER BOOKS
P.O. Box 690
New York, N.Y. 10019

Please send me the books I have checked. I enclose a check or money order (not cash), plus 50¢ per order and 50¢ per copy to cover postage and handling.* (Allow 4 weeks for delivery.)

_____ Please send me your free mail order catalog. (If ordering only the catalog, include a large self-addressed, stamped envelope.)

Name _____

Address _____

City _____

State _____ Zip _____

*N.Y. State and California residents add applicable sales tax.   11

27 million Americans can't read a bedtime story to a child.

It's because 27 million adults in this country simply can't read.

Functional illiteracy has reached one out of five Americans. It robs them of even the simplest of human pleasures, like reading a fairy tale to a child.

You can change all this by joining the fight against illiteracy.

Call the Coalition for Literacy at toll-free **1-800-228-8813** and volunteer.

Volunteer Against Illiteracy. The only degree you need is a degree of caring.

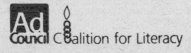

Ad Council   Coalition for Literacy